RetroGirl

Pemmican Publications gratefully acknowledges the assistance accorded to its publishing program by the Manitoba Arts Council, the Province of Manitoba – Department of Culture, Heritage and Tourism, Canada Council for the Arts and Canadian Heritage – Book Publishing Industry Development Program.

Design & Typography by Relish Design Studio Ltd.

Printed and Bound in Canada.
First printing: 2010

Library and Archives Canada Cataloguing in Publication

Thompson, T. D. (Twila Dawn) 1953-
Retro girl / written by Twila Thompson.

ISBN 978-1-894717-57-1

I. Title.

PS8639.H643R48 2010   jC813'.6 C2010-901413-8

PEMMICAN PUBLICATIONS INC.

Committed to the promotion of Metis culture and heritage

150 Henry Ave., Winnipeg, Manitoba,
R3B 0J7 Canada
www.pemmican.mb.ca

 Canadian Heritage   Patrimoine canadien

 Canada Council for the Arts   Conseil des Arts du Canada

 MANITOBA ARTS COUNCIL
CONSEIL DES ARTS DU MANITOBA

 Manitoba

ENVIRONMENTAL BENEFITS STATEMENT

Pemmican Publications saved the following resources by printing the pages of this book on chlorine free paper made with 100% post-consumer waste.

TREES	WATER	SOLID WASTE	GREENHOUSE GASES
7	2,985	181	620
FULLY GROWN	GALLONS	POUNDS	POUNDS

Calculations based on research by Environmental Defense and the Paper Task Force.
Manufactured at Friesens Corporation

Mixed Sources

Cert no. SW-COC-001271
© 1996 FSC

FSC

RetroGirl

T.D.Thompson

For Marion and Frank, whose sense of humour
and perspective still light my days

ChapterOne

Horrible though my day had been, home-schooling – a night-mare scenario that had been threatened more than once over the past couple of years when my days at school seemed to threaten my skinny grip on reality and scare my parents – would be even worse. 24/7 with Mom leading the so-called class. And a class of what? Cute boys? Girls I'd like to hang out with? Interesting persons I just might learn something useful from? None of the above. Me, that's what! Just me. And Mom, of course. I shudder to think.

But when my English teacher, Mrs. Collins, who up until now had been firmly rooted in the Precambrian era, came back from her Mazatlan vacation where some irresponsible but, I'm sure, well-meaning IT oaf taught her to surf the Web and use e-mail, I began thinking staying home with Mom might not be a complete negative.

Mrs. C., normally gray and almost invisible, is now all gnarly and computer-literate and forcing the whole class to start a blog. Sigh. And, not only that, but forcing us to Facebook her as a 'friend,' so that we can message our blogs to her inbox, thus maintaining a semblance of privacy. Double sigh. It's so demeaning being coerced by those in the position to do the coercing, to follow the herd this way.

And, plus, she's got a picture of herself on there. I checked. She's wearing a huge flowered hat and she's sitting on a beach somewhere and I am only grateful there isn't a picture of whomever was actually taking her picture. Probably some skinny old bald guy in plaid shorts and black dress socks. Gross.

According to her, this exercise will 'unleash creativity' and therefore it won't be marked, but used simply as a 'tool,' whatever that might mean.

The blog must be personal and descriptive. Sentence structure has to be complete. It must be about something affecting our lives. Right now! This very minute! It must be dated and it must be told in our own words. And it starts tonight.

Facebook: Between you and M. Collins
01-06-Yearofourlordwhatever

HOMEWORK-BLOGGER UNDER PROTEST a.k.a. H-BUP (I just didn't have the energy to think up a good title for this blog. Sorry Mrs. C., but, meh.).

Please Note - Registering Protest: It's hard to ignore the fact that you, Mrs. Collins, in addition to random unknown others who may have access to this blog, will be reading my innermost thoughts. Hence I must insist Mrs. Collins, and whomever else is reading, that I write this under protest. And that although you have stated, have *promised*, that our fellow classmates will not be allowed access to this blog, I remain unconvinced, which may in turn influence my choice of topics in this blog. Just saying.

You told us to describe our families for you. Brace yourself. And now, let the blogging begin:

Ahem . . . I have a mother. She's insane. I have a father. He's barely there. And then there's me. That's my family. As far as things affecting me today? Right now! This very minute! There isn't anything. I live in a void. End of blog.

Whoa. Who knew she even had any idea of how to access Facebook, let alone actually respond and then respond so bluntly. She put a smiley at the end to soften the whole thing and make like she's my friend, but I'm not that gullible. It was there so she could practise being a computer geek. She thinks icons are fun. She wants more details. She wants a window into our lives. She wants to insert her presence into our inner-most depths. Or so it seems, but anyway she definitely wants more. And that's just what she's gonna get.

Facebook: Between you and M. Collins
01-08-Yearofourlordwhatever

OK, then, you said you wanted more detail, so here goes. My mother talks to fairies. Not the gay kind you might be thinking of, but the ones who live in gardens and forests, under leaves and between the gnarled roots of ancient trees. The kind who wear dresses and hats made from the petals of flowers, and pants sewn from the long deep-green leaves of lily of the valley.

When it rains they balance a big oak leaf umbrella over their heads for protection. When it's really hot, they prop a purple and yellow columbine flower on top of their heads as a shield against the sun. They gather the satiny red petals of poppies and sew them together to make dancing skirts. The tiniest petals from marigolds become patches for the knees of children's worn-out clothing.

For transportation purposes they harness bees as horses, flying around in a blur of fairy activity with their buzzing steeds, hair flying in the wind, sun glinting off the dewdrops in their hair. Or at least, that's how I see it and how I was describing it to her this afternoon.

"Don't be ridiculous," Mom snorted. "Talking to fairies?

That's not what I do!" Chiding me is one of her main hobbies. She 'tsk's with the best of them.

"I mean," she continued, "maybe there are fairies. Who's to say? There could be, I suppose, and lots of people do believe in them." She caught me rolling my eyes at that point and stated triumphantly, "Arthur Conan Doyle believed in fairies and sprites! You know, the guy who wrote all the detective stories? You saw some of them on TV with Dad. About that detective . . . and his friend . . ." She trailed off. Mom tends to get a little 'absent' once in a while and our conversations are often like this. One-sided and a little hard to follow.

"He did!" she exclaimed when I refused to rejoice with her. "And lots of other well-known people do, too. I just can't think of their names at this exact moment." She gave me an appraising look and then said, "But honestly, Ariadne, this imagination of yours really needs to find an outlet. Why don't you go do something useful?"

That's it for today, Mrs. Collins! Ttyl.

Facebook: Between you and M. Collins
01-13-Yearofourlordwhatever

So, evidently that wasn't quite enough to fulfill my contractual obligations to this blog and the hope that I will pass English 10. You seemed to think my description of my home life was a little 'flighty.' Therefore, I carry on:

When Mom begins describing the voices she hears, the ones that rule her life, I basically do all I can to tune her out. She's totally old, as you would know, since you've met her at parent-student-teacher interviews. She says she's 39, but I've never seen concrete proof and personally, I think she's a lot older. Numerical age means nothing anyway, as she keeps pointing out to me in an attempt to prove that no matter how ancient she is she's still 'hip,' which only goes to prove my point, since 'hip' is something she's not now and has probably never been.

Here's the real proof that age is only a number and means nothing: I'm 15, if you don't get too technical about actual birthdates and so on, and I have more sense than she does. Scary isn't it?

I'm only jerking her chain when I talk to her about her crazy ideas, but she takes it all very seriously. She points out that her "gifts" as she calls them are what put meals on the table and shoes on our feet.

"Why can't we just use seedpods for shoes," I asked her innocently. "Why can't we simply gather leaves and sew them together with threads made from spider webs?"

That's the point when I saw her actually having to hold herself back from smacking me*. The only thing that stopped her is her conviction that whatever happens in this life is something she'll have to come to terms with in the next. She's determined to keep her karma as clean as possible because the last thing she wants is to have to deal with me again in her next life. It's such a laugh, really, because she's as trapped by her beliefs, weird as they are, as anyone else is. She's not free.

* Footnote: Just so you know, Mrs. C., Mom **would never** actually 'smack' me. She's a keen non-violence advocate, if you know what I mean: the kind of person who'd rather talk you to death than beat you to death. So, in other words, please don't call the cops or social workers or anything. The violence implied in the above sentence is strictly there for colour, so you don't get bored reading all this junk.

There. If that doesn't make Mrs. C. happy, then I have no idea what will. It's all there. Highly Personal Stuff! Gory Details

About My Disturbed Home Life! Things I prefer people to not know about me and yet, things that aren't all that awful. There's no way I'm trusting anyone, let alone a teacher, with the real stuff that goes on in my life. There's no way I'm describing to her how although my mother sees herself as a free spirit, flitting around the world, reading people's auras and cleansing their energies, she's basically full of crap.

I'm the free one. I'm the one with my whole life ahead of me once I'm old enough to actually leave this insane asylum behind and be on my own. I'm the one with the potential of finding real friends and a life outside this goofy house, once I manage to locate someone interesting who can accept me under my own terms, since I have absolutely no intention of groveling to anyone or of changing in any way. I'm the one who swings out the door every morning to a world miles removed from this place.

Actually, my life is mostly outside this house since bringing my friends over, once I actually get some of course, and then having my Mom wander out in her ankle bracelets and clinging long skirts is not something I want to subject them to.

Nobody else's mother wears tie-dyed draping skirts that whisper over the ground, long dangling earrings festooned with beads and feathers, hennaed hair down to her waist and bare feet with toe rings and ankle bracelets no matter how cold it is outside.

Nobody else's mother has teary-eyed strangers tapping at her door day and night, arriving with arms full of invisible psychological baggage and questions about their past and future, which they pay her to answer for them. Nobody else's mother has a mob of invisible chatty spirits hanging around the house whom she confides in, laughs with and asks advice from. Nobody's!

And none of it is anything I intend to go around sharing with the regular kids I go to school with. Being a loser is bad enough; being a loser with a crazy mother is even worse.

Chapter Two

Facebook: Between you and M. Collins
01-15-Yearofourlordwhatever

You asked us to describe what challenges us. I'm assuming
by that, you mean what things drive us crazy. For me, trying
to make and keep friends is my toughest challenge at this
point in time, which you as an observant older person may
have already noticed. And the fact they made me skip Grade
4 hasn't helped. Being the youngest in class every single year
makes me feel a little like everyone's kid sister or younger
cousin. I'm either the class pet, like some sort of human
hamster, or I'm ignored. Neither of these inspires confidence.

The only reason they skipped me in the first place is
because Ms. Baker caught me with a copy of *Wuthering
Heights* hidden behind my math book, decided I was way
smart, and passed me on to the Grade 5 class. If she'd
asked, I could have told her I was having a hard time with
the story. Joseph, the old servant guy in it, is incredibly
annoying and almost impossible to understand. I was only
hauling it around because Mom had absolutely refused to
let me read it until I was older.

Making me skip Grade 4 was a bonehead move. No offence
Mrs. Collins. Plus, the teacher in question was pregnant
at the time, and a little off her game, so to speak, so she

probably didn't give the whole thing as much thought as she should have. She sighed a lot. Got tears in her eyes for no reason and practically spat your name when she was ticked. Which was often. It was not a good year. Probably led to a lot of internal scars, if you know what I mean. Is this what you meant when you asked for what challenges us? Hopefully. Because otherwise I have no idea what you mean. Have a great day, Mrs. C.!

Mom tells me, on afternoons when I'm too exhausted by the trials of my day at school to fight her off any longer, that the people in my life are the ones I need to learn "life lessons" from in order to gain soul growth, so in the future I'll be a more highly evolved human being. Even the ones I don't like. Or, maybe, especially the ones I don't like.

Which is when, if I can summon the energy, I point out to her that her presence is actually my biggest challenge, not the presence or non-presence of my friends, and that the only thing I'm learning from her is how completely insane a grown woman can be without actually being hospitalized for it.

"Ariadne," she'll sigh in a tut-tut sort of way, "intention is everything. Please be attentive to the words you speak."

"Ari," I always correct her. "Call me Ari."

"Fine, dear." At this point you can see her visibly pull herself together, her palms floating upward to accept the messages from her angelic buddies. "Intention, Ari, please remember your intention in this world is everything."

"Mom, I have homework." And then I'm gone. Off to my room to hide from her.

In other words, I'm determined to give her a run for her money – an opportunity for her to prove herself. I like to think of it as her test in this life if she insists on putting that kind of spin on things. Maybe one day she'll find her soul has grown so huge from having dealt with me that she'll find herself thanking me for being a brat, and I'll become in her eyes someone other than the royal pain in the ass she thinks I am now. But I doubt it.

When I cave and tell Mrs. Collins that making and keeping friends is my toughest challenge, it would be misleading to make it sound like I'm totally bereft in the friendship department, completely a loner, totally single digit all the way, all the time. I mean, maybe I am, but not all the time! Not 24/7 or anything. It's more that I don't have any actual human-body-type friends – the kind with pumping hearts and a working central nervous system. Not currently, anyway.

As a child it was different. I had my pick of friends. Granted, nearly all of them were imaginary ones, invisible to the naked eye, but still they were a lot of fun. They were loyal and they were always available – something you can't usually say in all honesty about your average garden-variety-type friendship.

In addition to the imaginary ones there were a few real ones, like the boy next door. Kenny. We were total buds together. Hung together, ran races, played ball. His dad moved out first, then his mom took Kenny to the reserve to live with her mom and we got new neighbours – ones who weren't related to shamans on their mother's side, so of course they wouldn't associate with the likes of us. It's been a barren landscape since then.

Facebook: Between you and M. Collins
01-20-Yearofourlordwhatever

Interests. You asked about our interests. Well, I like shoes. The more expensive the better. I like soft red leather boots, maybe with a little fringe or some metal studs at the top or something. Zippers drive me to distraction. I love them on anything, and the more the merrier. I like really well-made flats, the ones you just know were handmade in some remote European country where they have to pay the workers more than the minimum wage, so the shoes are worth a week's pay for normal people here and only really wealthy people can afford them. And spike heels, particularly really steep pointy-toe ones that could become weapons on the wrong feet. I cannot get enough shoes. And boots. Biker boots with buckles, zippers and studs. I like them, too.

My interests are wide and varied; they include cute little skirts, the kind you can barely sit in, and those tiny tops with offbeat pictures and sayings on them that hover just above your belly button that you can layer and play around with. Long, droopy boyfriend jackets. Gauzy little tops that sort of flit around like wings and clothes that are made from hemp and bamboo.

 Not that I actually own any of these things. My clothing choices are a lot more limited. The stuff in my closet runs the gamut from some freaky '80s throwback shirt with a button-down collar that Mom found at a "really good price" down at the local flea market, to a skirt she's cut down and remade for me from one of her rejected floaty things. She's actually been known to come home completely thrilled, and expecting me to match her mood, after finding a plaid madras jacket with a stand-up collar dating from the Nehru fashion era. An era which, if you want my opinion, probably lasted about five minutes back in Mom's youth when rock groups were known mostly for hanging around with some crazy guru on mountaintops in remote parts of India or Nepal.

And that pretty much covers my *interests*, k, Mrs. C.? G'night.

Mom is the main breadwinner in our family, and the money she earns reading people's energies and predicting what spooky stuff their guardian angels are going to tell them to do is pretty minimal. Dad is her live-in secretary and the original computer nerd. He writes her newsletters, takes care of balancing the bankbook, and he tries to protect her from the really creepy people she tends to attract. Also, he does a little origami work on the side, which he sells at farmers' markets and along the street every summer during the local rodeo. Not exactly a big money-maker.

In other words, we have no money. We're poor and it shows. Believe me, it shows. Our house is what you might describe as 'ramshackle,' if you were in a kindly sort of mood – full of old furniture, patched duvet covers and mismatched dinner plates other people were getting rid of. Long swaths of pale blue fabric float around the window frames instead of drapes, since actual drapes cost too much. Mom, in a fit of creativity, sewed silver stars in random patterns on them a few years back, and some of the stars are a little frayed at the edges now. The floors are hard-wood, ancient and uncarpeted. They splinter easily, and if you're not careful a flame from one of the dozens of candles Mom keeps burning can singe you in places you're not prepared for.

A person can't bring friends over to a place like this without some kind of explanation for its oddness, particularly not the kind of friends I'm hoping to attract. It's too embarrassing. Just try explaining to the really top-notch girls (who can afford to be choosy where friends are concerned) why there are piles of salt at every door and under every window. "To keep the bad vibes out," Mom tells me, but it's gritty when you step in it by accident and nobody else has drifts of salt around their doorways.

Facebook: Between you and M. Collins
01-22-Yearofourlordwhatever

Hobbies? Today, you suggested we write about hobbies.
Evidently some of us are having problems fulfilling their
English 10 blogging requirements. Not me, of course, but at
any rate if you want hobbies, hobbies is what you get.

Currently, my main hobby is boys. Any kind of boys basically, but particularly the ones that every other girl in
school is wild about. The ones who are slightly dangerous, a
little outrageous and crazy. Not, I repeat, not the scholarly
types. Please do not see this as an invitation to match me
up with Roger Deakins. I know he's your favourite; everyone
knows that. But he's not my favourite, and I do not want
anyone matching me to anyone in any way no matter what.
Take this to heart, Mrs. Collins!

That's it. I'm not writing any more about this. I don't care
what this does to my final mark. Sorry. TTYL.

To me boys are what foreign soil was to the ancient Romans:
something to be conquered. But in my case, only after learning
all the little quirks that make them vulnerable to invasion. I'm
biding my time, basically, waiting for the day when I understand
those boys and know what magic makes them tick. I've been
biding my time for years.

Which brings me to my master plan. There are in my school,
as in every school in the world, a group of girls who are like boy
magnets. There's really nothing special about these girls that I
can see, but they have a way of laughing or tossing their hair, or
whatever, that seems to really get the males of the species on
their toes. I want the males of the species on their toes. I want
them high on those toes and going after me.

I need to learn the secret stuff these girls do, but I don't have any actual money to spend learning makeup tips and stuff like that. Nor do I have time on my side, since I realize I'm getting older every day and missing opportunities right and left. My only chance is to somehow make friends with one of these girls and learn from her. Maybe she'll feel sorry for me and loan me stuff. If I could make friends with one of them, somehow manoeuvering her into a strong enough sense of camaraderie that she'd loan me a pair of great jeans or something, I think I could actually get ahead in my plan.

The big problem, the huge boulder in my path, is my mother. If she knew I was even thinking any of this stuff she'd have me brainwashed by some cult expert before I knew what was happening. If she even suspected me of having any of the abovementioned interests she'd be wrapping me in cotton and shoving me in a closet somewhere until the interests wore off. Worst of all, she'd be lecturing me every living minute about karma and auras and the undead until I was ready either to scream or knuckle under to her manipulative tactics. Or, even more horrendously, actually start to believe them myself.

Therefore, all must remain secret. All must be done behind her back. On the sly. Which is not an easy matter when you're dealing with a woman who makes her living as a psychic.

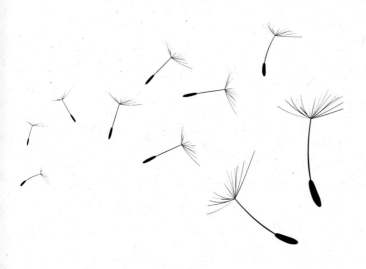

ChapterThree

Mrs. C. Facebooked me back, telling me she also had problems making friends when she was young and I shouldn't worry about it, things would work out just fine. OMG!!!! Does this mean I'm doomed to become her? I'll grow up to be a teacher surrounded by teenagers all day long, covered in dust and cobwebs from hanging around schools my whole life?

That is so not going to happen. The horror of it all is clear and my mind is made up. It's time to break out of this slump I've been in since forever. I'm making friends and I'm making them fast. There is no way I'm going to be a younger version of Mrs. C. for one second longer. Ick.

I have a plan. Admittedly, it's not a great plan, but it's better than nothing, and the fear of ending my life like Mrs. C., besieged by principals and crazy parents and needy people like me, is so terrifying it makes me feel like one of those guys who throws himself over the edge of his foxhole in a war movie. Sacrificing myself and exposing my lowly rank just to get it all over with.

Dreaming my way through math this morning, the path to acceptance and popularity in school suddenly became crystal clear. Those girls I had my eye on had so many options open to them they'd probably have to be forced to become my friends. In other words, they were gonna have to owe me something. Something major. They were going to have to be bought. Problem was, there wasn't much they didn't already have. Except my friendship of course.

"Hey, Deena," I whispered. I was filled with sudden inspiration. "Lend me some paper."

Deena's a little like me, definitely outside the main loop of things, but she's nice, in a "see-you-later-can't-stop-to-talk-now" kind of way. In other words, she's OK if there's no one else around, but she's sort of an Einstein, and a little bit older, and she'd take a mighty dim view of the plans I had for school domination if she caught wind of them.

In some ways she seems a lot different from most of the kids around me, so I'm thinking she flunked out and had to repeat and that's why she's so serious, but at the same time she's really smart and it's hard to see how anyone that smart would flunk. Deena's confusing that way, but let's face it, I haven't spent that much time trying to figure out why she is the way she is. If there's ever anything really serious going on she's a good one to talk to, but at my stage of desperation and with the plan I had in mind, she'd be no help at all. I knew this instinctively.

"And a couple of those pencil crayons," I added. "Good colours, please."

She threw an irritated glance at me, but bent to search through her backpack anyway. She'd been taking notes like mad while the teacher went through some intricate mathematical concept, which no one in their right mind would ever have to use in the real world outside of school tests, and I knew she was worried she might miss a step or two by helping me out.

"It's OK." I tried to ease her mind. "I'll keep listening for you."

That thought didn't exactly seem to reassure her though, and she emerged from the search through her backpack with flushed cheeks. She flung her entire set of pencil crayons at me and snapped, "Here, take them! Now be quiet."

Even Mr. Steed – math teacher though he was, and thoroughly engrossed in his subject – even he seemed startled to awareness by her vehemence. He paused for a second and looked at us questioningly, one eyebrow raised. I'm convinced he thinks the raised eyebrow makes him look rakish and young, but really it only makes him look slightly under the influence.

"Sorry, Mr. Steed." I spoke up, always ready to take a bullet for the team. "I was only asking Deena for a little help with the theorem. You know," I continued, "so I could do well on the test and all, and you of all people must realize I need to do well on all my tests, so I can get into a good university later on in order, of course, to make a decent living, buy a car, get a house, have a kid or two . . ."

The whole class was staring at me now and I realized babbling like this wasn't going to give me an edge on finding friends among the popular girls, so I flourished a piece of paper in the air with a stab at devil-may-careism and smiled at Mr. Steed in what I hoped he'd see as a friendly way.

"Interesting concept, though." I couldn't seem to stop myself, and a certain part of me was standing back in horror at my own blabbiness. "All those numbers, all those little pluses and minuses and brackets and stuff. Interesting how they all tie together. Colourful. They're colourful little things."

Most of the class was staring back at me now, the majority of them resentful at having been wakened. There were a couple of giggles and a few groans. Shut up! shut up!, shut up!, my mind was hollering at me. Just simply sit still, put your paper down, look at the desktop and shut up. And so I finally did.

Facebook: Between you and M. Collins
01-27-Yearofourlordwhatever

I realize, Mrs. C., that we probably weren't supposed to even work on this blog today, since you didn't come up with any demands in class, however I want to set the record straight, because our last little blogging episode has got me totally creeped-out. And I mean that in a good way, so don't go

all teacher-crazy on me. Just to put your mind at rest, I
do have friends. Honest. Or at least I will in a few days.
Please don't worry about me not having any friends. Please
don't tell anyone anything. Please keep everything totally
hush-hush.

Not that I think you're talking about me in the teachers'
lounge or anything, but things do have a way of leaking
out. Schools are absolutely primed for worming people's
deepest secrets out of them. Just saying.

And thanks. Thanks for keeping all this between us. But
if you have any really good ideas about invitations or the
kinds of random things people might do at sleepovers, it'd
be totally cool if you share them, since I basically have no
idea. If indeed, you had sleepovers back in your day, which
you probably did, since there was no doubt a lack of other
fun things to do. No computers, no IPods and the movies
were black and white, as well as pretty lame, judging by the
ones they show on the oldies channel, so sheer desperation
might have made a sleepover way more of a big deal for
you. So what on earth did you do at them?

My brain was totally fried. This was completely foreign
territory for me, this friend-making or actually, if the truth be
told, friend-purchasing business. The invitations, for example,
were going to have to be extremely unique: unusual, colourful,
different, something that would catch the eye of say, a Brandi or
a Tiffani, girls who were used to looking at all the latest fads with
a jaundiced eye. Those kinds of girls were not easily impressed.
It wasn't even a sure thing the simple sleepover I had in mind
would do the trick; I'd probably also need really good stuff to eat
and something to drink other than tap water. As I laboured over
my first efforts there in math I realized I was probably going

to need something tempting, something that in turn would no doubt end up costing me actual money, in order to lure these girls into friendship with me. One huge obstacle would be the fact that I now had precisely a buck twenty to my name.

I scared up two dimes, a nickel and a couple of pennies from the bottom of my locker, but there was no hope of any more cash coming my way in the immediate future. Not unless I went out and got an actual job or something, and there was really no time for that. Plus, how desperate can a person get? At the same time, even stickers, even Life Savers or gum cost more than what I had. There were six girls I had my eye on for potential influential friends. They were the elite of the school; my measly cash outlay was not likely to impress them

The other pressing issue was timing. I was going to have to swing this sleepover while Mom was away. She had one of her seminars in weirdness planned for the next weekend, meaning she'd be gone for two full days, busily leading the easily-snowed into believing they were seeing ghosts and communicating with the dead.

'While the psychic's away, the non-psychic will play' – that was my motto. Dad would automatically go along with absolutely anything I wanted to do, of that I was virtually certain, and, knowing him, he'd be so distracted in his own little world he wouldn't even notice me sweeping up the salt and blowing out the candles.

Normally Dad wanders around in some dimly lit universe of his own, singing little songs to himself, humming as he folds his papers, giving me hugs and generally listening to mom's viewpoints without offering many of his own. And he seems happy. Although how anyone could be happy who's actually married to her and living in this crazy house is absolutely beyond me.

He's very highly educated, although nobody would guess it to look at him. Those ancient T-shirts he refuses to throw out and that frayed bathrobe that he wears for days at a time over a pair of old pajama pants make him look like some sort of derelict, but in fact he's got his Master's degree in Philosophy. It's not exactly a money-making, in-demand type of profession obviously, and this hanging around the house, not going to an office, just making origami sculptures and manufacturing Mom's business cards and newsletters, is his chosen way to thumb his nose at the mainstream world of big business. Or so he says.

The important thing is, he's a pushover when Mom's not around to straighten him out. He likes things peaceful. Sleepover time with Dad around was bound to be laid-back and remarkable mostly for his non-interference.

Facebook: Between you and M. Collins
01-29-Yearofourlordwhatever

You asked us to describe our day. Really? It's so boring. You must be running out of topics.

But since you asked, it was later on today, at lunch, when I was doing my usual gig standing in the hallway trying to look like I didn't mind standing in the hallway, that I saw them. My holy grail, so to speak. There must have been people like this back in your school, too. You know, the really shiny ones who have everything.

To protect their privacy and also because too much information can be dangerous for both of us, I'll just say there were two guys walking along talking and laughing and having a good time and behind them, right behind them - matching them step by step - two girls walking and talking and having a good time. They were obviously together, the girls following their guys; they were the cream of the crop, exactly the same, only different. The girls were bleach blond and skinny with their makeup and their thin legs, strutting, and the boys were so cool in their faded jeans and their attitude like the hallway belonged to them and no one else.

Those couples represent precisely what I envision for myself. Precisely what I am aiming at and seeing them only reinforced my determination to make myself one of them. If it kills me I'll be part of their group, and I'll do it before spring break.

To make it stick I went so far as to make a silent vow right there in the hall. I spit into the palm of my left hand. Not a lot, you know, just a little bit, and really casually made an "x" in the spit, rubbed my palms into each other and shoved my hand into my pocket. There. I'm not sure how much you know about the supernatural, Mrs. C., but nobody can undo a spell like that one. Even Mom, freaky though she is, would have to respect a vow like that.

"Deena," I whispered. "Got any money?"

The withering look she shot over at me would have been enough to discourage most people, but as you are aware, Mrs. C., I pride myself on not being like most people.

"C'mon, Deena," I said again. "Just a dollar, even? Or two? I can pay you back." Some day, I thought. I was careful not to be too specific. A lot of people like to be paid back before the dollar drops any further in value.

Deena purposely squirmed around where she was leaning against her locker until her back was actually to me. She didn't even have the common decency to say no to my face. It was disappointing because I'd thought she had more backbone than that, and it was really too bad because Deena was basically my only chance at borrowing any cash.

Nobody else in this horrible place was quite as easygoing and gullible as she was, of that I was certain.

Ack. Forget that I said 'horrible.' Honestly, it's not that bad here. Sometimes. And you said we should be honest, so I'm being honest! Don't hold it against me.

Once again, I have to emphasize that this blog remain personal! Just between us! Honestly, if I'm being completely open with you, I have to say Mrs. C. that getting some of this stuff off my chest is liberating. In some ways you remind me of my imaginary friends back in my child-hood. That's a good thing, by the way, not creepy like it might sound to you. Anyway. Math awaits. TTYL!

ChapterFour

Later on, when I had time to think about it, I realized it was probably for the best that Deena turned me down. It would take a whack of cash to impress the girls I was hoping to impress. A whack of cash I'd be unlikely to pay back to whomever loaned it to me, thus screwing up yet another aspect of my already hideous life.

My days at school are pretty quiet ones. A lot of people don't even bother to answer me when I do manage to find the guts to speak to them. Even Deena, and believe me, she has no right to be so picky. In a weird way I kind of enjoy the silence, to be honest. It gives me time to observe people, which has been my main hobby ever since I can remember. Kind of like collecting butterflies in the old days, but without the little pins. Or the actual death throes.

Fortunately for me I do enjoy my own company, and all those voices inside my head make it seem sometimes as if I'm in the middle of a crowd anyway. Which also seems to be another thing that seems to set me apart from those who swim in the mainstream, those whom I'd now decided I wished to join. Most of them don't seem to have any more than one voice in their heads – their own voice, obviously. I have a crowd. A crowd that often disagrees with each other. Makes it interesting though, listening to all the dissenting voices.

As someone who lives so far off the beaten path herself, Mom has spent an inordinate amount of time making sure I live a sheltered life. She never comes to school for bake sales or any of the other mother-infested special events, and since I've never been chosen for a school team, she's never been tempted to appear at tournaments and cheer me on. We've kept our private life extremely private and, don't get me wrong, I'm not complaining about that, but it's made it a little tough to figure out how to fit in with the mob who've spent their formative years fighting on the local playground and establishing a certain number of ground rules.

All I really want is for her to act like other people for a change, so that I can be like regular people for a change. If she'd just start dissing a few of the other moms, for example. Complain about the teachers. Criticize me and suggest that maybe I'd better lose some weight, or use some makeup or dye my hair, like the other moms are always doing to their girls. Act like a normal human being, is all.

I mean, I'm just saying. It'd make my life one helluva lot easier. And that's another thing: she won't allow even a tiny bit of swearing. And believe me, you cannot take the Lord's name in vain in any way at all, because even though she says it's not really a big male god in the sky, it's energy and light and all that crap, even then if you start swearing at all, she's just totally freaked by it.

Facebook: Between you and M. Collins
02-02-Yearofourlordwhatever

Sigh I know we don't have English again until tomorrow, but maybe you've heard how all my sleepover invitations were returned with variations of "sorry, I've got plans," and "sorry, I've got surgery" and "sorry, I plan to do anything possible to avoid you." It was discouraging. It was demeaning. It was an eye-opener.

Not that I want to dump this on your shoulders, Mrs. C., but
if you had problems making friends way, way, way back in
your day, then how did you solve it? Was there a certain
thing you guys did back then that made sleepovers really
fun events that everyone wanted to attend? Maybe you
didn't have TV then, so people were more desperate for
things to do. Did you even have radio? You didn't just sit
around and read books or anything, did you?

Or did some miracle occur? Did you grow into a fiendishly
cool person overnight and everyone fought to be friends
with you? Is there something I'm missing here? Because,
obviously, I'm missing something.

That's repetitive. Sorry. Never mind. Don't worry about
it! Forget I even mentioned it, because this is pretty lame,
asking for advice from a teacher. Once again, no offence or
anything. I'll figure out something. 'Bye.

In my foolish optimism it had once seemed possible, even
likely, that the six girls I had my eye on would love to come to
a sleepover at my place. Sleepovers sounded like fun, although
I'd only done them with cousins at my grandmother's house,
but it seems they were now way too immature for girls of this
calibre. All I could do was kick myself for having not been cool
enough to realize this. Obviously there was an overpowering
need for more drastic action – something really big to grab the
attention of the half-dozen in the group, or the "G6," as I'd come
to think of them.

"Deena!" I caught up with her a couple of days after all my
invitations had been completely dissed. "Whatcha doin'?"

It was a move meant to disarm. Like it or not I needed
Deena's help. My days as a lone wolf in the school were over
and I needed at least one person on my side. The choice was

made. It was makeover time, and I was now obsessed with a semi-destructive desire to purge the old me and come up with a brand new one.

Deena pulled to a halt, her arms piled high with books. "Why?" she asked in what could only be called a suspicious way.

"Nothing. Just thought we could hang for a while."

"Oh." She seemed a little confused. Maybe even flattered, although I don't know why she should be.

I am, at the very least, an extremely ordinary person in every way. Nobody ever takes a second look. I have straight, boring brown hair that falls to around my shoulders, a stupidly romantic name that I've shortened to "Ari" in an effort to appear less of a doofus, no figure to speak of – straight as a stick, as they say – and I get average grades. There's nothing of note about me. I do have nice eyes, blue eyes, and those are the only things about my face that I honestly like. Otherwise, I'm bland. I'm also moody and I have this inborn tendency to get really depressed and down on myself, but once the moods have come and gone I'm like a total steamroller of energy and brilliant ideas.

A long session in front of my mirror the night before had convinced me there was at least one area of myself I could change. And that's where Deena came in.

"Want to get together after school today?" I asked.

"I guess." She shrugged. She seemed too surprised by the request to actually refuse.

"I thought maybe we could go to the drugstore first," I began. "You know, just to take a look around and stuff."

"OK." Deena took her free hand and tucked a chunk of hair behind her ear.

She has the strangest face. In one kind of light it's sort of interesting, all planes and angles and kind of little-girlish, as if she needs to grow into it. In another kind of light it's just plain homely. Her nose is too big, her chin is too pointed and her hair is completely horrible in a chopped-off-in-a-moment-of-insanity kind of way. Her eyes tilt a little, like almonds, but she rarely looks at a person square on and it's difficult, once she's out of sight, to remember what her eyes actually look like or what colour they might be. For all I know they might be two entirely different colours, and that wouldn't surprise me in the least, because Deena, quiet and studious though she is, is one of the strangest people in school.

Facebook: Between you and M. Collins
02-10-Yearofourlordwhatever

Thanks, Mrs. C, for all your concern. I shouldn't have written that last post. Sorry, once again, to drag you into this, but I mean, after all, you're the one that started this whole insane blogging thing, so in some respects it's sort of a 'meh, too bad for you' time. If you know what I mean. So then today you asked all of us to write about our friends. I hope you realize most people are going to censor themselves pretty severely on this assignment! Good luck, though.

But speaking of 'friends.' Poor Deena, so desperate for friendship she was even willing to settle for me. We're friends now. She may not realize, but we are. And don't get all concerned and worried about it. I don't really feel that sorry for her! She's alone in the friendship department too, and so this is for her own good. This way she can have at least one person at school to sit with at lunch.

Not that I'm that terrible. Maybe I don't have terrifically high self-esteem, but I do have my good points after all, a sort of mindless optimism (which I must have inherited from my Dad) being one of them. You haven't met him.

He goes to school events even more rarely than Mom. He leaves that to her. He says it's his allergies, but we both know he's kidding. If you're wondering what he's like, just think of my mother and then double the weirdness factor and imagine someone even less involved in real life. That'd be my Dad.

That wasn't really about friends like you'd asked. But it's about the right length. You asked for a couple of paragraphs and this is more. Adios!

It was OK to pretend with Mrs. Collins that I had Deena's best interests at heart, which of course I did. Sort of. But at the same time, it was lucky for me Deena was so desperate. She has a way of standing back in school and watching everyone else. She's a loner, but there's more to it than only the fact she's unpopular like I am. In her case, it's more like she chooses to be alone. It's like she's got a pair of invisible, warm arms wrapped around her that make her totally cool on her own, so she doesn't need anyone else. As if she's in a gentle bubble – untouchable and contented. It's so weird. I don't know how she can feel that way, when in my case being a loner is synonymous with being a loser. Deena's a little hard to read, but I figured it was time all that changed. We needed each other. Or at least, I needed her, which in my head is basically the same thing.

That afternoon, at our lockers after school, I pulled her obviously reluctant arm out and tucked my hand into the crook. Buddies. That was us – good buddies. I beamed at her and she rolled her eyes and struggled to free her arm, but upper-body strength is one of my main traits, and I held on until eventually she stopped fighting.

"See? Nice to be buddies, isn't it?" I'd thought it was a good conversational topic, since we clearly had nothing to actually talk about, but she only glared over at me.

"Let me go!" she snarled through clenched teeth.

We were on our way out of school at that point and several groups of kids had stopped to watch us pass. Jealous. I knew they were only envious of our budding friendship, but Deena didn't seem to think so.

"Get your hand off me," she whispered. Her voice was hoarse, with embarrassment as it turned out, but at the time I was a little concerned.

"Coming down with a cold?" I asked. "You know, a little Vitamin C is great for 'curing what ails you,' as my grandmother says." I chuckled in a stolidly "buddies forever" kind of way. "Grandmothers," I mused, "quite the characters, aren't they?"

"OK. Let go of me." Deena was turning out to be quite the little fighter. "People are laughing at us. Let go!"

Laughing? Maybe I hadn't been reading the mood of the crowd quite as well as I thought. It's one of those gray areas Mom says I need to work on. She feels I don't follow my intuition, don't listen to the spooks she insists are trailing along behind my shoulder, and generally don't pay the proper attention to life and its mysterious karmic happenings.

She's probably right. I disentangled my arm from Deena's and lifted my chin a little higher. Give 'em the right attitude and these kids would be eating out of my hand. Trouble is, I never seem to hit on that right attitude. I seem to always somehow slip past, sliding into a no man's land of missed opportunities and misunderstanding.

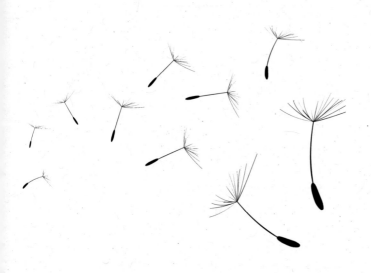

ChapterFive

Later that night I sat at my kitchen table and watched as Mom's chin hit the floor. It isn't easy shocking her. I mean, this is a woman who deals with ghosts and dead people all the time. She talks to the dead. The *Dead*. Like I say, it isn't easy getting her attention.

"Ariadne," she moaned, "what have you done?"

A simple little change in my outer look. She should have been more concerned with my interior and my intentions. Even I knew that.

"Mom," I said gently, "the inner me hasn't changed."

"I know." She dropped her head into her hands and rubbed her thumbs over her eyes. "That's another problem altogether."

Well, thanks. I mean, thank you very much. She was not only insulting, but probably correct as well.

"Who's this Deena you've been talking about?" she asked. "Is she the one behind all this? What's her mother's name?"

"Deena's mother has nothing to do with this," I stated emphatically. I wasn't even positive Deena had a mother. She never talked about her family. As far as I knew she lived alone in a pod somewhere. A really intelligent pod. She hadn't needed to be home for dinner like I had; she'd been hanging around there at the drugstore as if she had all the time in the world.

"Mom, I needed to do something, or I'll never get any friends," I began reasonably enough. "Never. Besides, I think it looks kind of cool and different. I needed a big change."

"Your hair," she said slowly, as if she thought maybe I didn't understand English anymore, "is polka-dot. I've never seen such a thing in my life."

"You mean in all your life*times*, don't you," I chided gently. This was obviously going to take a lot more getting used to than I'd originally counted on. Mom's own hair currently hangs almost to her waist – long and straight and a sort of copper colour at the moment.

"I feel my hair is an extension of my personality, Mom," I said, hoping to appeal to her on a level she'd understand.

"Your personality is polka-dot?"

"It'll grow out. Eventually. And it's not 'polka-dot.' It's actually a soccer ball." I riffled one hand through the little pentagonal shapes that covered my head.

"But it's so short." She seemed almost ready to cry. "Your beautiful hair."

"My hair was never beautiful," I said. "It was boring. Capital 'B' boring, Mom. This is different. This'll really get me noticed. Nobody can ignore me anymore; even the popular girls will see me now."

"Oh, Ariadne," she moaned. "You don't even like soccer. When have you ever played soccer? When have you ever even played any sport? You're a sitter, Ariadne, you like to sit and think, or sit and read, or sometimes draw, or just, you know, *sit*."

This was true, I had to admit. I am a sitter. A watcher. Standing back, out of the action and observing the world as it goes by is something I'm proud to say I really excel at, and I enjoy it, too, so she had a point, but at the same time she was missing by a huge margin the motivation behind my actions.

I was actually beginning to feel sorry for her. It can't be easy when you're a middle-aged mother, stuck there in your rut no matter how abnormal it is, whose daughter has begun to spread her wings and fly off into all those wide-open spaces you left behind long ago.

"Mom," I began, "I know it's got to be tough watching me blossom."

"Blossom?" She gave a strangled kind of laugh. "Ariadne, if this is your idea of blossoming I hate to think of what's going to happen when you start to wither."

I threw her a disappointed look and immediately, as I knew she would, she began worrying about her karmic energy. At these mother-daughter times I can almost read her mind. She was sorry she'd laughed at me, sorry she'd been so negative regarding my emotional well-being, sorry she'd forgotten to call me Ari, sorry she'd ever gotten pregnant with me in the first place.

One time, when I was really small, I'd been watching her get Christmas dinner ready and she'd accidentally dropped a freshly baked pumpkin pie, face down, on the kitchen floor. She'd stood and gazed at the gloppy, orange mess for a long moment and then said in quiet, funereal tones, "I wish I'd never got married." I know how her mind works in these situations

"I'm sorry," she muttered. The bangles on her arms glittered and clashed together as she raised her hands and made a temple with her fingertips in front of her face. "I'm truly sorry, Ariad . . . Ari. You know I only want you to be happy."

"I know Mom." I rushed in before she got all carried away talking about how important I was to her and how thrilled she was with having me as a daughter and all the other blah, blah, blah stuff. "And this makes me happy. Really."

Facebook: Between you and M. Collins
02-11-Yearofourlordwhatever

Everyone's been staring at me all day. I know it's the hair, and I know it's a little 'out there,' but it makes me happy and that's what's important, right? Well, truthfully speaking, not happy exactly, but not depressed either. Sort of thrilled I found the courage to make myself over so dramatically, but a little worried about what other people are thinking. It can be pretty unpredictable, the behaviour of one's peers. And although Deena seemed to think I looked if not great at least interesting, I realize that her reaction is certainly no guarantee the G6 will see things the same way.

('G6' refers to the girls I want to be like. The half-dozen gorgeous ones in school. You know them. They're mostly OK students, and they're heavily into yoga or Pilates, lots of mascara and dyeing their hair blond. They usually have boyfriends, they all hang out together. You know?)

But to carry on, in my attempts to explain it all to Mom, the whole sordid story began sounding just a little peculiar. It isn't going to be easy swinging her middle-aged mind around to the type of logic I'd been following when I got this haircut. And I'm not sucking up when I say, Mrs. C., that I don't think your mind is nearly as middle-aged as my Mom's. You hang out with kids all day, whether you like it or not, and that's bound to affect you, so I'm sure you'll get it when I say all I'd been hoping to find was a very cool colour that Deena could help me with.

Things didn't work out that way. It'll grow, though, right?

When I hatched the original plan, I'd been anticipating an evening spent at Deena's place, the pod as it were, with the two of us experimenting with my hair, and me eventually walking out with a shining curtain of, say, Autumn Honey Gold or Platinum Baby Ash or whatever. A totally new human being. Someone brimming with endless possibilities. Just like the models on the covers of those boxes.

Instead, we'd hung out at the cosmetics counter, gazing at the numbing variety of hair colours, Deena acting bored out of her skull, as if being with me was practically killing her. She kept mumbling about homework and essays and math questions until I finally nearly shouted at her, "Deena, stay on track here! We're here for me, remember, we're going to do a traditional girl thing and make me look gorgeous!"

At which point Deena had thrown me a long, calculating look and said, "And you have what exactly? Twenty-three cents in your pocket?"

"That was last week," I said, "I now have about five bucks."

Dad had proved to be an easier touch than Mom, and on the weekend I'd donated some time running spell-check for him so he could e-mail her newsletters. For this favour he'd emptied his pocket and scrounged a few lost quarters for me. He'd wanted to spend the time experimenting with a new pattern for a flying swan he was hoping to sell.

He uses the roll ends of wallpaper samples to construct his designs – feeling, as he says, that the heavily embossed stuff projects the most ambience, and thrilled at the same time that the ends of rolls are often free. It's sad really, but kind of touching at the same time, how whenever he comes up with some new design he gets totally excited, figuring the world is his oyster, so to speak, and people will simply flock to him with money clutched in outstretched hands, begging to buy his stuff. I have to respect his eternal optimism, but at the same time, that optimism isn't producing any actual cash.

The woman behind the counter almost laughed in our faces when she overheard us. She'd been watching us for the past half-hour like some kind of evil hawk eyeing her prey.

"I'm sorry, girls," she said in an overly sincere tone that simply smacked of sarcasm. "There really isn't anything you can buy at this counter with that amount of money."

Bright red nails matched her bright red mouth. Miniscule blobs of lipstick had gathered in the corners of her lips, bobbing around as her mouth moved. She wore gloppily mascaraed lashes and a thick mask of pale foundation. It was fascinating, really, attempting to locate the real person underneath the layers of makeup. Sort of like watching a living archeological dig.

Deena dug an elbow into my side as if to alert me that I'd been staring unnecessarily. The woman's eyes narrowed.

"Girls," she said, "if there's nothing for you to purchase here, perhaps you'd best be moving along."

A nastily polite way of telling us to get lost.

"We wouldn't want to tempt you into doing anything that might get you into trouble, now, would we? Any problems with the store management and police can stay on your record indefinitely."

She hadn't actually accused us of being there to shoplift, but the sentiment was clear. In her eyes Deena and I were nothing but potential thieves, and something in me boiled at the thought. Not to speak for Deena, because truthfully I have no real idea of what kinds of acts she might be capable of, but I do know myself. And I happen to know I'd rather be drawn and quartered than steal some measly little hunk of crap from the cosmetics counter of the local drugstore, which after all is basically only a grubby little hole of a place and not exactly the Ritz or anything.

I may have said something along those lines to the woman, because the next thing I knew Deena was hustling me down the shampoo aisle, her face beet-red with what I assumed was humiliation.

"Sorry," I mumbled. "Didn't mean to . . ."

"No," she gasped. She clapped a hand over her mouth, her eyes glittering. "That was great!" she enthused. "Fantastic! She had it coming. What nerve!"

OK. So in other words I hadn't managed to alienate the one and only ally I'd been able to find. A little bubble burst in my chest and I started to laugh, which is when the rest of my afternoon turned upside down. It never fails. As soon as a person, meaning me of course, feels she's done something the least bit brave or shining or even right for a change, something else comes along to screw it up.

In this case it was a stock boy who turned the corner, rolled a metal trolley into the back of my right knee, and neatly knocked me into the pile of conditioner bottles he was planning to shelve. This one careless move sent the whole box of containers spewing all over the aisle. Neon green bottles careened under my feet. They rolled into the little groove place under the bottom shelves. A couple ricocheted up and knocked some shampoo down. The racket, and a long burst of laughter from Deena, garnered an evil glare from Red Lipstick Lady – who had followed us to the end of the aisle – but to my relief, nothing more.

And Deena and I immediately dropped to the floor and fell all over ourselves trying to help the guy pick things up again.

ChapterSix

"**H**ey, thanks," the guy droned in a kind of slow drawl. He seemed less than concerned over the incident. "Would've taken me all afternoon to pick this stuff up."

I got the impression that falling conditioner bottles, falling anything bottles, was a pretty routine occurrence for him. Not only that, but it seemed clear to me that shampoos, hair colour and beauty aid stuff in general were quite low on his personal list of things to spend time thinking about. He also seemed to have lost sight of the fact that he wouldn't have been in this mess if it weren't for him smacking that cart into me in the first place.

I rubbed the back of my knee and watched as Deena tossed another bottle back into the box, then sat back for a moment and shook the hair back from her face. She was dressed head to toe in black, as she always is, and her hair, a long tangle of deep brown, stuck statically to her T-shirt.

"Hey, Deena!" the stock boy cried suddenly. He sounded surprised and at the same time ecstatic. "Hey, what's up, babe?"

Babe? This sounded interesting. And not, I might point out, what one would expect when shopping with Deena.

"Hi, Eric," she mumbled.

Her cheeks were scarlet now, and I cradled a couple of bottles in my arms and sat back to watch with fascination. The guy looked at least 10 years older than us, and he was scruffy in an unshaven kind of way, but clean. It was obvious he cared about how he looked and he smelled really good, not perfumey but sagey like the potpourri Mom uses. He wore what looked like a tribal symbol tattooed on one wrist. There was an air of independence emanating from him, a kind of electricity that brought out a little corresponding electrical impulse on my part, one that hit with an unexpected and not entirely comfortable tingle. In addition to his obvious physical attributes, Eric the stock boy was obviously thrilled to see her and not scared to show it. Deena was proving to have unexplored depths.

"Deena, where you been keeping yourself?" I thought he might actually hug her. "I missed you. I didn't know where to find you. I asked Joe and then Carl, and nobody knew where to get you. Where you been keepin' yourself, girl?"

This was too weird. He seemed to be over 20 and was slightly unkempt, in what was, as I continued to gaze at him, an extremely attractive way. He had a little pointed beard and one ear was pierced with a small silver ring. His dark brown hair was pulled back into a ponytail that hung halfway down his back. One eyebrow had another plain silver ring through it, and there was a glint in his eye that gave his appearance a sort of frightening aspect. Frightening in the good, shivery sense of the word, not the scary, lecherous sense. I could only sit back and watch silently.

"Well," Deena cleared her throat, "I've been around . . ."

Even to me she seemed to be dodging the main issue. Where had she been? What had she been up to? Other than school of course, where I'd been sitting next to her every day since September. And why hadn't this rather strange older stock boy-type character been able to find her when he so obviously wanted to? The questions bounced around inside my head as I watched her feeble attempts to dodge this guy's questions.

And the "guy," as I refer to him, was actually continuing to improve upon inspection. Not only did he have a little beard, which let's face it, none of the boys at school were able to conjure up yet, but he had a certain mystique roving all around him. As if he was a stock boy by choice, because it left him lots of free time to dream or something. Or as if he felt working for a living was beneath his dignity. A little like Dad, I had to grudgingly admit. Or as if he was living a whole other life in his head and this one in the drugstore was only to put food on the table to enable him to continue to support his dream life.

He stood there, a couple of lonely bottles rolling around his feet, and waited patiently for Deena to finally answer. The look of expectation on his face was the same one I could feel on my own. This girl was turning out to be more than the simple brainiac I'd always assumed her to be. How she even knew anyone as slightly disreputable as this guy was simply beyond me.

"I've been around," she answered, obviously uncomfortable. "You know, going to school, stuff like that."

"Yeah, but," he lowered his voice, "I've got this crick in my neck, man. I just can't get rid of it. I tried everything." He sounded slightly aggrieved. "You weren't there. I can't go to just *anyone*, and nobody knew where to find you."

Deena shot a look in my direction and then glanced nervously toward Red Lipstick Lady, who had her eye on us from the corner of the passage. "We can't talk here," she mumbled.

The guy turned and glared down the aisle, and Red Lipstick twisted on her heel and headed back to her counter.

"They can't fire me," he said reassuringly. It seemed he knew what Deena was thinking. "Nobody else knows where I put the stock in the back. Nobody else can read my writing, and nobody in their right mind wants to work here in the first place."

For the first time he glanced down at me, where I sat, bottles of conditioner still cradled in my lap. "Who's she?" he asked, nodding in my direction.

"A friend." Deena sounded secretive, as if she was unwilling for the two of us to be aware of each other. "A friend from school."

"School? That's great! I always said you should go back and get your high school. Whatcha gonna do after that?"

As if a person had a choice. What on earth could he be talking about? I was already getting the third degree at home about my so-called future.

"Maybe college?" Deena was so completely ill at ease I was surprised this stock boy guy couldn't see it. "I don't know," she faltered.

"Cool." He nodded, his pointy little beard going up and down. He bent and took the bottles from me and placed them gently on the shelf.

"So when can you come over and fix my neck? We've got a new place," he continued, "and you haven't even seen it. Joe's there," he added helpfully. "So's Carl. Even Jen's back."

"Well," Deena was hesitant, and I knew it was all my fault. I was definitely the unwanted third party in this situation. However, being third party has never really bothered me in the past, at least not enough to make me actually leave, and so I stayed – ears open, eyes wide, waiting to see what would happen next.

"C'mon," he wheedled. "I gotta get this thing fixed. It's keepin' me awake at night, man."

Deena glanced over her shoulder and then at me. "Not here," she whispered urgently.

"Well, then, come over to the house," he said reasonably. "Everybody'll be glad to see you. You can have supper. In an hour, OK? I'm off in an hour."

"I can't." Deena shot a look at me and I took the hint.

I pride myself on my innate ability to read a situation and instantly respond. In this case I could see that 'Babe' Deena was incredibly uncomfortable and desperate for a way out. Just call me obliging, but I figured the least I could do was lend a hand, since the only reason she was here in the first place was to help me.

"We've got to do my hair," I volunteered, and at his appraising look, I said, "You know, just make some minor improvements."

He was silent. "Maybe a different colour?" I added. "Possibly some waves or something?"

"I'll do it," he said.

Do what? For a moment I was completely at a loss for words, a state of affairs, which I have to point out, doesn't often occur. Even Deena seemed stumped.

"Do what?" I asked reasonably.

"Your hair." He lifted a strand and dropped it, then took both hands and ran them through my hair from temples to the back of my head. "Something different, I think," he mused.

"We'll need to make your eyes stand out," he continued, "because you really do have beautiful eyes. You shouldn't hide them. And great cheekbones."

Absolutely no one had ever run their hands through my hair like that as far as I could remember. I was absolutely certain no strange man had ever done it in the shampoo aisle of the drugstore before. It felt like something I could get used to.

Deena had an almost frightened look on her face. "No," she began, "we've really got to get going . . ."

"No we don't," I said

"No you don't," he chimed in.

This was the point in my story where Mom's eyes had literally glazed over, giving me the impression I'd probably once again indulged in a little too much detail for her liking.

"So we went back to his place and he did my hair," I finished cryptically.

ChapterSeven

Facebook: Between you and M. Collins
02-13-Yearofourlordwhatever

It's weird, I'm so used to blogging this thing, it felt like
something was missing this morning when I realized I didn't
have to write it. So I did write it. And now, this being Friday,
you, Mrs. C., can spend your weekend reading it. Revenge
☺. Kidding, only kidding! Maybe you don't even look at your
comp on weekends, but still the last couple of days were
such a struggle I figured I'd tell you about it.

You know about my altered looks, obviously, since you've
seen me at school, but even though you said you thought
my hair was kind of 'rad,' you have no idea what a struggle
it is at home to get any sort of approval. Remember how I
said Mom wasn't crazy about the whole hair-cutting deal?
That was an understatement. She was not only furious, but
also imagining all kinds of scary possibilities. That woman
has way too much imagination. All of it focused on me.
She's liable to put me under lock and key for the next 10 to
20 just to make sure I don't do anything like this again.

My question is . . . What did you do back in the day when
you ticked your mother off? You must have, because
everyone does, but what did you do? How'd you get her

to trust you again and to give you a little freedom? And respect? I'm missing out in the respect department, big time! Because ultimately this entire situation centres around respect, of which I get practically none. The more I think about it and write about it to you, the more I realize that's really the issue here! Respect. Huh. Who would've guessed.

Well, thanks again, Mrs. C. Have a groovy weekend!

"OK . . ." Mom's voice was a little strained that day, after I explained the original concept to her and gave her a chance to talk. I could tell it was taking all her strength to fake calm. "So you went to this stock boy's, this *stranger's*, house and he did *this* to your hair?"

She was becoming a tad shrill, and I waved a serene hand in the air. "It's OK, Deena was with me. I didn't go there alone."

"And he's how old? Twenty-five you said? What on earth is a 25-year-old man doing with a girl like you?"

Well, thanks once again. Thank you so much for the compliment. For a long moment I just sat there, shocked at her lack of faith in me.

"I am not even going to dignify your insinuations with an answer," I said finally, my tone conveying what I hoped was a calm aloofness.

It was what she deserved, even though I did feel a bit guilty. In her place, I grimly conceded, I'd probably feel the same doubts. However, it was high time she started giving me some credit for having a little common sense. "And I never said he was 25, I merely stated he was a little older."

She leaned forward and peered at me over the top of her glasses. "OK," I added grudgingly, "maybe he only looks like he could be 25. He's probably only 22, maybe 21." I was reaching here. "Maybe he's 19. He has a very cute little beard.

"And besides," I added with a certain snide asperity, "don't forget my 'guides' are with me all the time."

She drew in a sharp breath. "Ariadne, we both know your guides are constantly by your side, but they are only as effective as the amount of attention you pay to them. You need to listen to them," she urged. "You need to disconnect from the little, tiny, unimportant three-dimensional world around you and specifically tune into the next dimension past this one. Detach. Take yourself a step away from who you are! You have to become one with the spirit of the universe and actually leave your current self behind."

Well, I had already suspected what nutty stuff she was going to come out with, so simply tuning her out was the easy part. Besides, Eric had been a perfect gentleman and not interested in me in the first place; even I could tell that. He was so thrilled at having rediscovered Deena after what seems to have been some long-forced separation that he could barely take his eyes off her. His roommates, once we got to the house, were just as bad.

Deena and I rendezvoused with Eric in the alley behind the drugstore half an hour after our run-in with the conditioner bottles, and I basically tagged along at their heels as they strode off into a part of town I'm normally ordered to stay away from.

The drugstore we'd been shopping in is across the street, a block down from the school, and there are trees in the boulevard and a little playground across from it. Next to it are a couple of boutiques and a coffee shop where Mom sometimes does readings, but only a couple of blocks farther along, the ordinary stores start to give way to tattoo parlours and adult stores, the sidewalks get pitted and there's an old hotel that always looks like it's ready to be condemned and put out of its misery. Rusting grocery carts line the back alleys alongside the dumpsters, and there's a hair salon with a big handwritten sign in the window offering cheap massages.

The house they were headed for was a tiny, dark affair just behind an ancient grocery store, next to a place offering second-hand goods and free soup for transients.

It's a tough-looking neighbourhood with a defeated air about it, as if the residents had long ago given up any hope of improving their lives and were only biding their time waiting for a miracle or their own death to change their circumstances. It's a neighbourhood Mom is always warning me against. The houses are small and mostly the kind of dented, unpainted and curled-up-shingles kinds of places everyone suspects are full of drug dealers and their pals. Of course, most people don't realize the main drug dealers are living in those huge white mansions out on the edge of town in the new neighbourhoods. Handy to playgrounds and schools. They can afford it, after all.

Gladdened cries filled the shabby little living room when Deena walked through the door, and I could only stand back in amazement. This was the girl who if anything was an even bigger pariah at school than myself. An achievement, by the way, which is not to be taken lightly.

"Hey, Deena! Deena-girl, where ya been?" The happy cries of Eric's various roommates still lingered in my ears as I faced Mom across the kitchen table.

There had been a time-consuming round of hugs, kisses on the cheek and various greetings of the kind usually reserved for those newly back from the dead. The experience had been remarkable mostly for its humiliation as I, and my hair needs, which after all had instigated this whole reunion in the first place, were consigned to the far back burner.

I stood there in the doorway, one hand sort of gripping the other, one foot digging its way into the dirty carpet by the front door, feeling my cheeks redden to the point where even my ears felt hot, as the gladdened cries went on and on.

Let's not forget this was the same Deena whom most of the kids at school seemed barely able to remember from one day to the next. The same Deena who sits quiet like a captive rabbit through our classes, who never raises her hand, who drifts silently through doorways and sits with her books and papers near her in a tidy pile, never spreading them all over the desk and floor like most people do. It's as if she wants to be able to disappear at a moment's notice, leaving nothing behind her except possibly a wisp of energy, a shadow of smoky self.

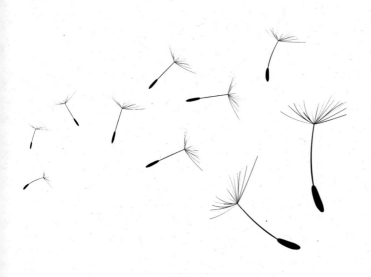

ChapterEight

"**W**ell, my goodness dear," Mom began, my new hairstyle obviously forgotten for the time being. "Why don't you bring her over sometime? Your guides have brought the two of you together for a reason, don't forget that."

Yeah, yeah, I'd heard it all before. The reason was my hair, Mom. I knew better than to say it out loud, though. She'd be off on one of her "our guides are our friends" rants within seconds, and there was still more to tell her. The way I saw it, I had the floor here and I had every intention of hanging onto it as long as possible. It's not often I get anyone's undivided attention.

It's not that I'm selfish or anything; I'm just filled with a basic human need for constant reassurance and attention. It's a need I have a terrible time fulfilling. It's basically a curse, and I'm hoping someday I'll outgrow it. However, having Eric drape a slightly damp and musty-smelling towel around my neck in the kitchen of the little house, and then being told to sit, to simply breathe and to trust him to handle my hair came close.

The kitchen was characterized mostly by its air of squalid intimacy; the smells of last night's dinner still hung like a murky cloud in the air. Someone had obviously in the recent past burned the onions. A pile of dirty dishes was heaped in a haphazard fashion in the sink, spilling over onto the counter. A dishcloth, still damp from previous use, with a slightly mouldy tinge sent out a rancid, foul smell like a little bacterial bomb ticking away on the side of the drain board.

Normally I don't notice these sorts of things, but with Eric's hands in my hair, stroking the strands out from my scalp, massaging the roots, trailing along the tips of my ears, it was either concentrate on externals like the horrible kitchen or give in and start purring like a cat with a dish of cream.

Which would, of course, be highly inappropriate and also incredibly humiliating. So I concentrated on staring at a chunk of peeling wallpaper while Eric made conversation with Deena and the others.

"You gonna do my neck then?" he was asking.

I could feel Deena's eyes gazing speculatively at the back of my head. "Sure," she said quietly, as if to herself. "I can do that."

"Great!" Eric's exuberance was in direct contrast to her hushed voice. "'Cause it's drivin' me absolutely friggin' crazy. Can't do anything, man. Hurts all the time. Only thing that makes it feel any better is weed, and I stopped spending my money on that, so now nothing helps. Carl's into meditation, so I'm gonna try that next."

He was using a razor on the back of my neck now, and through the buzzing some of their conversation escaped me, but the gist of it seemed to be how Eric had decided drugs were too expensive and he'd given them up. Not to mention he was mad at whomever normally supplied him. Deena's responses were so quiet I could have kicked her. Speak up! my mind yelled silently, Can't hear you! She was oblivious and seemed to be purposely speaking even more softly than she normally does, no doubt to keep her conversation with Eric a private one. It's a situation I'm not unfamiliar with. A stab of jealousy rammed through me.

How was it Deena managed to acquire a set of friends like these – cool, older people who seemed to really like her – while

I was relegated to futile attempts at impressing the G6? How unfair was that?

And when the razor finally stopped and Eric stepped back to general oohs and aahs from all and sundry, I was left there, the musty towel still pinned around my neck, while he and Deena disappeared into a back bedroom.

Not that I blame her, you understand, but it was still an unsettling position to be left in. Everyone else had sort of straggled off at that point and I was abandoned on my chair, clumps of hair on the floor all around me, no mirror in sight, no broom either and no way of making myself useful by cleaning up. Not that I normally care about things being terribly clean, but it seemed the least I could do under the circumstances. There were mounds of hair all over the place.

And the voices I could hear from the bedroom next to the kitchen were hardly reassuring. There was a low murmuring, which seemed in my fevered imagination to go on for hours. Then there was a long period of silence and a sharp burst of laughter, which I immediately recognized as Eric's. Deena was not only proving to be a person with unimaginable secret friendships, but also a bottomless pit of the kind of possibly sleazy behaviour up until now only dreamt of by myself.

Mom's eyes were rolled so high, they were nearly popping out of her forehead by this point in my story and I finally decided I'd told her enough. If she wasn't going to respect my narrative capabilities, then she could just forget about hearing the rest. And, besides, I was basically done anyway.

"You know, Ariadne," she began, "Deena and Eric may have been doing something totally innocent in that back bedroom. Civilized people do not condemn others rashly. They weigh the odds, look at the *facts*" – I cringed at her emphasis – "and even then the enlightened person strives to not judge others. If we judge," she carried on, "we become judged in return."

It drives me nuts when she makes so much sense. I hate it when I'm forced to admit she might be right.

"Fine," I said grudgingly, "but what else would they be doing? Why was Eric laughing and how come Deena's so secretive about everything? All that talk about his 'neck.' I bet its code or something."

Mom's bracelets jangled as she placed her palms flat on the tabletop. "I'm getting a very strong feeling about Deena," she said softly.

She was looking straight into my eyes with that penetrating (but a little bit dopey) gaze that comes over her face when communications start coming at her through the ether. It's an unfocused but intense stare, and it's one more thing about her I've never been able to wrap my mind around. It's impossible for me to meet her eyes when she does this, and the hushed voice she uses when under the influence of her messages sends me round the bend with frustration.

All I really want is for her to behave normally, talk in a normal tone of voice, wear normal clothes, go shopping for things other than restaurant-size boxes of salt, and bitch with her best friend about the other moms behind their backs. In other words, I only want her to fit in with other parents the way I want to fit in with other kids.

"You know," she was saying in a slow singsong when I finally tuned back in, "I'm getting that Deena has strengths she's unaware of. Or . . . no . . . She is aware of them. She's frightened of them, and at the same time, she's honoured. She's following a long tradition. I can see masks. She's hiding.

"Wait a minute!" There was a note of excitement in her voice. "Now, I see bows. Lots of them! Pink ribbons, satiny ribbons, the ends falling, cut in an inverted vee, beautiful bows . . ." She was silent then, her head cocked at an angle, craning her neck in an attempt to gather in her ghostly voices better.

"Gifts. She has gifts . . .," she murmured. "And love, she's full of plus signs, positive signs. Pink is for love. Such a pretty colour of pink around her," she mused.

Mom paused again and then focused her eyes directly into mine. She asked, "Does Deena ever talk to you about receiving messages from the other side?"

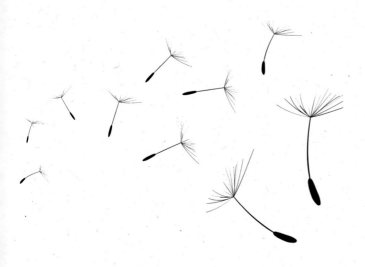

ChapterNine

Facebook: Between you and M. Collins
02-17-Yearofourlordwhatever

There's a lot to be said for living your life inside your head; for never coming out into the real world and having to deal with the real people in it. Mostly those real people are annoying, and also they can be generally so insensitive to the feelings of people like myself, who may be slightly different, that it's positively discouraging to see how narrow-minded the majority of the population seems to be.

At the same time, there's a lot to be said for being a part of that vast sea of normalcy. One of them being the ability to blend in to the faceless ocean of humanity in the average school. Just saying.

I thought you'd be interested, because I'm figuring this is a genuine insight and so you, as a teacher and so forth, will probably realize that I'm making progress. Not quite as dense as I was a month ago, for example.

Were we even supposed to blog you today? You didn't mention anything, but maybe I wasn't paying close attention either. Anyway, there ya go! An insight for you.

"Ariadne." Mr. Steed's voice was like a steel trap, breaking crudely into my thoughts later that morning. Math. I hate math. "The answer please, Ariadne."

"Eric," I blurted, without thinking.

As the sounds of laughter from the rest of my classmates echoed through the room I wanted to crawl under my desk and die. Not only that, but there is an actual Eric in my class, who was now sitting there smirking at me like someone who just punked his best friend.

"I didn't get that one," I mumbled.

Not only did I not get it, but I'd had more sense than to even attempt to work it out the night before, when staring at my new haircut in the mirror and dreaming of Eric's hands on the nape of my neck had seemed far more important, but I didn't see any point in letting Mr. Steed in on that little secret.

My soccer-head hair had caused more than a minor stir when I walked through the school that morning. I'd actually caught myself earlier, tugging at the wispy bangs Eric had left drifting down over my eyes, hoping somehow to make them longer in order to give me a place to hide.

Mom, who had been sending me sympathetic glances all through breakfast, had offered to drive me to school, an almost unheard-of suggestion in a household where the ability to struggle off in the vilest weather imaginable was seen as the equivalent of those badges kids earn in Brownies. At the time, though, my courage was reasonably high and I was even a little proud of my new distinctive look.

All that changed when the school actually came in sight and a sort of general unrest began to boil up in the pit of my stomach. Vaguely similar to the kind of upheaval that hits once a month when physical aches and mental dread herald the onset of my period, that same sinking as if the bottom of my body was about to defy gravity and actually drop out of sight was hitting me as Mom drove into the school parking lot.

She'd picked the right-hand lot, the one reserved only for teaching staff. Naturally. Just part of her innate ability to ignore the common rules of civilization.

"You know," I began conversationally, "I'm feeling a little under the weather this morning. I hadn't wanted to bother you," I continued hastily, "because I realize I need an education, however . . ."

She hadn't even had the common courtesy to let me finish. "Ariadne," she said in her gentlest voice, the one she uses a lot with Dad, "I realize this is going to be a very hard day for you, but it's important for your personal growth to see it through to the end."

Personal growth, my left foot! "Mom." I'd struggled, but managed to keep a totally reasonable tone of voice. "I honestly think I'm coming down with something. There are a lot of flu viruses going around these days, you know."

Flu. The perfect illness. Such a wide variety of symptoms, some of them almost impossible to disprove.

"Now Ariadne." Mom had rolled to a stop in the spot reserved for the school secretary. Again: naturally. The secretary's spot, premium parking for the one person in the school with more actual power than the principal. "Struggle makes us stronger. You will grow and learn through your most difficult times. That's what the easy life doesn't offer: spiritual growth. You should be glad to be in a position where you'll need all your inner strength.

"Find your friend Deena," she encouraged when it became obvious I wasn't sucked in by her 'growth' sermon. "She'll stick by you."

"Fine!" I'd snapped, hauling my reluctant butt out of the car.

There was absolutely no point in admitting to her my major plan of eventually ditching Deena in favour of the G6. Even I, blinded though I was with dreams of being part of the top group in school, knew Mom would be incensed. And plus, I realized it was not the nicest thing in the world to consider doing, which made me feel a little disgusted with myself. Also, I was beginning to enjoy hanging with Deena, although we hadn't actually hung out that much and she was keeping a really tight lid on talking to me about anything. Still, she was kind of cool in a very odd and uncool way.

Which is how I found myself in math class, cowering behind my text and trying to ignore the amused glances of my classmates as well as the more concerned ones of Mr. Steed.

"Ariadne," he sighed now. His eyes turned to the ceiling and then rested on me again. "You didn't do the homework, did you?"

"Well, no."

"Well," he replied, "why not?"

"Well." I was willing to play the game as long as he was. "I was busy."

"Well, what were you busy with?"

By this point, of course, the rest of the class was hanging on every word, thrilled no doubt at the drama unfolding in front of them. Ready to grasp at any straw that would take time away from actually doing math. Except for Deena, whose concern was evident in her expression as she watched me from across the aisle.

"Well," I said, and I will admit my voice probably held a rather tense tone, possibly even slightly snarky, "I do have a life to live, you know, and math isn't always a part of that life."

"Well!" Mr. Steed's tone had changed too. "Perhaps you'd better stand back and take a long look, young lady, at the path you're headed down."

"Well, what path might that be, Mr. Steed?"

"Listen!" He was nearly shouting now. Apparently he'd abandoned our little word game, which was almost too easy a win for me. "If you're not careful you'll find yourself out on the street in a few years with no job! You'll have no money and even fewer prospects, young lady."

"And doing math problems at night is going to save me from that?" I was incredulous. How could he even pretend to believe what he was saying? "How is knowing some obscure algebraic formula gonna help me buy baby formula for that illegitimate child you probably envision me having?" My voice was rising and I seemed unable to bring it back to a normal level. "After I finish paying off my junkie, of course!"

I'd gone too far. His face was visibly throbbing now with suppressed anger, his cheeks had reddened and he reminded me of nothing so much as one of those cartoon characters right before they implode with suppressed rage.

"Ariadne!" And now he definitely was shouting. "The office, young lady!"

"Uh, Mr. Steed?" Deena's voice broke into the mist of animosity poisoning the air. "Maybe I should take her down there for you? Maybe she should be seeing the school nurse."

Nurse?, I thought, why a nurse?

"Nurse?" He seemed to be taken off guard. "Why do you think she needs to see the nurse?"

Deena sat, her hands pressed flat on her thighs, and faced him. "You have to admit," she said, "Ari's not usually belligerent."

Not out loud, she might have added, if she'd known me a little better. Behind the scenes, though, I was plenty belligerent. Outrageous, even. Obnoxious.

"So her unusual mood might indicate that something is physically wrong with her," Deena continued.

I was impressed. This girl was becoming a sort of bottom-less pit of hitherto unimagined surprises. First there'd been Eric, then that house full of slightly disreputable friends and now this purposeful misrepresentation to a teacher.

Mr. Steed was quite obviously nonplussed by this unexpected turn of events. He stood there, undecided, for a long second, then snapped, "Fine! Take her to the office. And then hustle right back here yourself, young lady!"

Chapter Ten

Mr. Steed's last jab was only to save face in front of the rest of the class. Anyone could see that. As he turned his back to me and started towards his desk, I shot Deena a look of sheer gratitude. She missed it, though, because she was bent over her papers, frantically jotting down last-minute notes.

"C'mon," I whispered. "Let's get going!"

Even the office was better than sitting there with the prying eyes of half the class watching my every move. Every strand of hair on my head was itching like a little antenna, shivering from the knowledge that they were the focus of all that attention.

"Deena!" I tried again. "C'mon!"

She stood with a heavy sigh and gathered her books into a neat pile. The look she threw over at me was more resigned than anything else. It was more the kind of look I'm accustomed to receiving from Dad, for example, than Mom.

"OK," she said finally when everything seemed to be tidy enough for her. "Let's go."

The office is a kind of still backwater of the school. A silently gloomy place with a slightly menacing air where people are sent to meditate upon their actions, ask forgiveness from the gods who rule the school, receive whatever sentence is deemed appropriate and then be turned loose upon the world to commit their crimes again. It's a system that's probably never really worked, but no one seems to ever gather the energy to question it.

To be honest, I had never been sent there in trouble before, and the idea of it was a little freaky. I envisioned bright lights in my eyes, unscrupulous ways of making me confess to crimes I hadn't committed, unidentifiable muffled sounds coming from behind closed doors. The whole TV-spy motif.

"You know," I said quietly as Deena and I walked the silent halls, "I'm not sure I want to do this."

"Do you have a choice?" Deena sounded amused. "Honestly, Ari, what got into you?"

"You don't have to do this," I said. "You could stay in class."

"I know." She sighed and shifted her books. "Look, we need to talk before you go in there."

She stopped and forced me to turn and look straight at her. "You listening to me? You have to pay attention. You can't go off letting other people know my business. Ever. So no talking to anyone in the office about me. Or any other kids about me. Or Eric! Or the house they live in! Understand?"

She waited for me to nod and then went on. "This seemed like my only chance to get to you before you start talking to anyone else. I know you can be a motormouth sometimes. So remember what I'm saying. My life is closed to anyone I don't choose to let in. Closed," she repeated. "Tell me you understand."

"Yes," I muttered, and when she kept standing there, I added, "I understand! My lips are zipped. Honest."

I wasn't sure what to add, and after a minute's silence she continued a little less intensely. "Ari, when we met Eric it was a total surprise to me. I had no intention of introducing you to any of my old group. I didn't even know where any of them were anymore. And that's what you have to keep to yourself. Promise?"

"Well, sure." What else could I do? Who would I tell anyway? "I told Mom," I confessed, "but she doesn't know anyone here at school."

"OK." She stopped and looked at me straight on. "Nobody else. Understand? My private life is private and I want to keep it that way."

"Yes. For sure." I mean, I got it. And to be totally honest, I wasn't that upset about not being able to share the story of Eric with anyone else anyway. Why would I invite competition? That would be insane.

Plus, it was good to have Deena's company as we headed into the office. They've tried to make the place less darkly intimidating, but it hasn't worked very well. Instead it's now a bright white kind of intimidating, but with Deena beside me I could actually pretend to be quite blasé about the whole experience.

It wasn't until the school secretary gave me the evil eye and mentioned calling my mother that I really started to worry. And not because of any reaction she might get from Mom, but more because of whatever reaction Mom's presence might cause in my school. Soccer-ball hair is one thing. Mom's whispering skirts, ankle bracelets, toe rings and arms raised in spiritual supplication are another.

"Uh, no," I said contritely. "No need to call my mother. I'll just apologize to Mr. Steed and go back to math, if that's OK with you."

The secretary was sporting a haircut that looked like someone had stuck a frizzy-hair helmet on top of her head, so it was difficult for me to understand why she narrowed her eyes in furious disapproval whenever she glanced at my own hair.

"Does your mother know you've done this?" she demanded.

Well, obviously, since my mother is neither blind nor stupid, has eyes in her head and has seen me since yesterday. "Yes," I said.

"And she approves of your behaviour in class?"

Who assigned her as the enforcer of this prison? "As far as I know," I said.

"Is she aware of how you've behaved in this particular class with this particular teacher?"

Well, she is psychic, but probably not quite that psychic. "Has someone phoned her?" I asked a trifle nervously. "Because if you've phoned her then obviously she's aware."

"Don't take that tone with me, young lady," she snapped back.

Tone? What tone? I glanced at Deena where she sat, arms folded, eyes gazing into some private space. There'd be no help from her direction.

"Sorry," I mumbled.

As if following my look, the secretary's eyes narrowed at Deena. "Young lady", she said in what can only be described as a semi-sneer, "I do not believe your presence is needed. You may leave the office."

She preened slightly as Deena opened the door and slipped out. The woman tapped her fingers on her keyboard and seemed about to jab me with another question, when the office door opened and Brandi was propelled through with a force that seemed excessive. Behind her was Principal Brockner, a terrifyingly strict disciplinarian whose rules of standard teenage behaviour seemed to have been forged in the Middle Ages. During her formative years. When she was still young. Before she grew the moustache.

I guess it was the half-smile on my face, which I had pasted on in an effort to appear conciliatory, which drove her over the edge right off the bat this time.

"Ariadne!" Brockner's voice rose to an irritatingly high note, kind of like those whistles certain types of anal people use for training their dogs to do all kinds of unnatural dog acts. The sort of shriek that seems to pierce your brain and nail itself into your brainstem. "Into my office, young lady!" she howled. "Brandi!" She pointed at a chair. "Sit here until you feel you can go back to your class."

And into the office I went – my proverbial tail tucked between my legs, my ears down, a slight whine at the back of my throat. Enough of the dog analogies. At the time, though, it's definitely how I felt. Like a soccer-ball-headed mutt on its way to the big 'farm' in the sky.

An extremely long 20 minutes later, I had not only apologized to the Headmistress of Principalship about a dozen times, but I'd also figuratively prostrated myself before the Shrine of Math-Teacherdom to the point where I was actually convinced that algebra would indeed make a difference to me in the years to come. The amount of brainwashing I'd endured was incredible. And easily undone later, I realized to my own relief, once I'd left the precincts and found myself back in those hallowed halls of learning, and on my lonesome trail back to math class.

Deena was nowhere in sight, and I assumed, after a quick glance through the main hall, she'd gone back to math. I was grateful, though, for her escorting me to the office and hopeful she'd never have to do it again. Low profile, I thought, keep that low profile, girl. In fact, normally I'm nearly as quiet and shadowy around school as Deena herself, and walking through the empty echoing halls was freaking me out just a little until I spotted my fellow sinner up ahead.

"Hey, Brandi." She was standing facing her locker, head down. "What's up?"

We were alone in the hallway, and because of our shared history back at the school office, I somehow felt we might have a bond. A bond I intended to make use of.

"You OK?" I asked.

She tilted forward and rested her forehead on the locker door.

"Everything all right?" I tried again. "Hey, so what about that Brockner Babe? She's just downright nightmare alley, completely Stephen King, hey?"

I waited, I mean, maybe I'm naïve or something, but I did expect some sort of answer sometime from her. I'm not that much out of the loop. Well, actually I *am* that much removed from the loop, but members of the G6 have been known to talk to me on occasion, and on this occasion there weren't even any witnesses.

"Brandi?" I tried again, and by this point her continued silence really had me concerned. "Can I do anything?"

I had this crazy idea it must be thoughts of her mother's reaction that were weighing her down. I know those same thoughts were certainly weighing me down.

"It'll be OK," I soothed, "your mom'll get over it. They always do. Some of them got in trouble in school too, and those among them who can throw their minds back far enough to actually remember their youthful sins are pretty forgiving."

"What are you talking about?" She had finally turned to face me, her eyes rimmed with red. "Why don't you just leave me alone?"

"I'm talking about your mom," I said rationally, "and how she'll get over you being hauled into the principal's office."

"Leave me alone," she said again, but her tone was quiet, defeated, and I decided to simply overlook her words. She probably hadn't really meant it.

"So," I began, "how do you like my hair?"

She let out something that sounded like either a strangled snort or a stifled sob. "Your hair?"

"Yeah." I riffled the little pentagon shapes. "It's a soccer ball," I added helpfully. Some people who weren't terribly sports-oriented seemed to be having a certain amount of difficulty figuring that out. "I had it done last night."

"Why?" She had finally looked at the top of my head. "Why did you do that?"

"For shock value, mainly," I said. To get you and your friends to actually notice me for a change. And, I thought a trifle smugly, it seemed to be working. She tucked a long strand of blond hair behind her ear and took a closer look at my scalp.

"Why are you so weird?" she asked finally after an appraising look at not just my hair, but all of me. "Why can't you be like everyone else?"

"Why would I want to be?" I asked, caught off-guard.

Truth be told, I was a little ticked. After all was said and done, if I was being honest with myself, I valued anything that made me stand out from the crowd, although I still intended to be part of that crowd. The plan was for me to become the unique, interesting person in the crowd.

"I kind of like being a little different," I admitted.

"Cool," she said, although she obviously didn't mean it.

"But seriously" – her tone became a little terse at this point – "if you acted normal you'd fit in better."

"Fit in where?" I asked reasonably. "Fit in with you guys?"

She looked uncomfortable, and I knew she was trying to figure out a way to tell me no without actually telling me no. I have a sixth sense about being dissed, and it was actively waving little feelers in the air at me at that point.

"Why are you hanging around with that girl all the time?" she said, changing the subject.

"Who, Deena?" It was a little flattering that someone of Brandi's stature had noticed. It seemed she and her gang would have more important, popular-group type stuff to occupy them. "She's nice," I offered.

"Is that her name? Yeah", she said, "the Indian chick. Why hang out with her? How desperate are you, anyway?"

Pretty doggone desperate if the truth be known, but that has nothing to do with who Deena is, I thought. "She's nice," I repeated. I cleared my throat uncomfortably.

It was difficult to know where to take the conversation next, since ultimately I'd never noticed Deena was Aboriginal or anything but simply Deena, and plus, I was now really pissed and a little afraid of saying something that would scuttle every plan I'd ever had about squirming my way into the G6. This was still my intention, although I had every intent on accomplishing it completely under my own terms.

"See ya," I said finally.

"Yeah," she'd turned away again and seemed to be struggling to keep herself together. Her shoulders were hunched forward, trembling a little. It seemed being bawled out by Brockner had really hit her hard.

"You OK?" I asked again. Her behaviour seemed a little extreme under the circumstances, and an instinctual urge to help her surged up in me. "'Cause really, if you aren't, then just tell me what I can do."

She was silent for a long minute and then, just as I was turning to go, very quietly, in almost a whisper, she said, "I need someone to help me, someone to talk to. Someone to take all this away from me. I want my life back." Her voice was quiet, but I thought I'd caught a note of fear.

"Your mom?"

"That's what Brockner says," she sneered, and now when she turned again to face me her features were distorted. "She's full of it! If I could talk to my mom, don't you think I'd have done it by now? Don't you?"

"Your dad?" I had no real idea of her personal situation, but I knew in my own case Dad could be a lot easier to face than Mom when things got rough. "Try talking to him."

"He's not a part of my life," she said in what seemed like a rehearsed answer. "He's gone."

Soothing upset people isn't really my strong point. My talents lie more in making others slightly pissed off, so I was definitely out of my depth here, but I've never let that kind of thing stop me before. I put one hand on her arm and looked her in the eye.

"Look," I said reasonably, "how bad can it be? What'd you do? Forget your homework?" I snorted in an effort to show how little a problem that was. "Lip off the teacher? Fall asleep in class? Big deal! Your Mom'll get over it!"

"Oh, god." She dropped her head into her hand. "Go away," she moaned.

And so I went away. I don't need to be told twice. I simply took myself and my cool new hairdo "away." Back to math class where I sat and mulled, mulling being something I'm good at, and entirely preferable to actually listening to Mr. Steed.

In fact, so deep was I in my mulling, it wasn't until lunchtime when I swam back to consciousness.

"Hey, Deena." She was on her way to her locker to get her lunch and I put a hand out to stop her. "Thanks for hanging with me in the office this morning."

She sighed and gave me an appraising glance. I smiled back in what I hoped was a sincerely appreciative manner, because in all honesty I really did appreciate her concern earlier. I'm just never sure what others are going to deduce from my facial expressions at any given time.

Like I said, the voices yakking away inside my head can get a little overpowering. Not only that, they often disagree, so that when I smile at someone for instance, like I was doing now, sometimes I end up questioning whether a smile is the best choice, which then leads to the smile drooping off into

no man's land while I start yammering away about almost any
subject just to fill in the empty space and to cover up the fact I
have no idea what I should do or say. The other person usually
ends up standing there wondering what on earth is happening.
Before I had a chance to start talking, though, Deena sighed
and spoke up.

"Come on," she said, "get your lunch and let's go outside."

ChapterEleven

The quad in front of the school consists of a patch of struggling ancient grass, dotted with a few enormous poplars planted by cowboy school kids at the turn of the last century or something, and a group of scarred and beaten benches. Every single square inch of turf has its own unwritten rules, of course and it's social death by ostracism to cross them.

These subtle niceties are, of course, simply wasted on someone like Mom, who chose that particular day to make an appearance at my school.

Deena and I had settled on a small triangle of grubby grass bordered by a curb running the length of the visitor parking lot. Not a pleasant place exactly, but since I normally wander the halls, nibbling a sandwich by myself, looking for someone to talk to, this was a definite improvement. Until I spotted her.

In reality, I had my back turned and didn't spot her so much as clue in to a certain murmur that swept across the crowded quad. A little shiver traveled down my spine. A sort of frisson of energy surged through me, tingling like a small electrical charge right to the tip of my ears, and some part of me knew before I could even turn my head.

"Oh, crap," I murmured. Deena had just opened her lunch bag and she shot me a questioning look.

"What?" she said.

"Do you see anyone kind of out of place behind me some-where?" My voice wobbled.

"What are you talking about?" Deena began and then stopped. "Oh," she said.

I knew it. My worst nightmare. Most people dream about being caught naked in public or something. That was the least of my worries. Being naked in front of a crowd of strangers was nothing compared to having anyone at my school get so much as a glimpse of my fanatical mother.

"Tell me it's not true," I moaned. I dropped my head in my hands, and pretended to be completely absorbed by what was in the bottom of my lunch bag.

"You must be Deena."

A worn pair of instantly recognizable sandals had stopped right beside me. A long swath of blue-green fabric brushed my arm.

"Hi," Deena said.

Mom was giving her a long calculating look, her eyes in that slightly unfocused gaze she uses. "We need to get together and talk," she said.

"OK." Deena, to my surprise, sounded cheerful, not at all what you'd expect from someone so determined to keep her physical and emotional space utterly unspoiled. In some ways, she often reminded me of a nature preserve, all pristine and free, and now her inability to truly grasp the depths of horror in this situation gave me a slightly different view of her. Somewhat less impressed if the truth be known, and slightly annoyed at her apparent lack of concern.

I pulled my head out of the lunch bag for a second and flung her a disapproving glance. 'Don't encourage her,' the look said. Then I felt Mom's hand on the top of my head.

Naturally. The one thing she could do to humiliate me further than she already had, and in front of absolutely everyone. She may be the psychic in the family, but even I knew the eyes of the entire school were on us. The sensation gave me the creeps, as if some long-lost family secret, which everyone had bent over backwards to keep hidden, and no one had talked about in generations, was about to be unleashed.

"I got a call from a Mrs. Brooker," she began.

"Brockner," I moaned. "Her name is Mrs. Brockner. Get her name right, Mom, please."

"Mrs. Brockner, then," Mom corrected. "She seems a little concerned about you."

"I'm fine," I mumbled.

"Well, that may be, but this Mrs. Breek . . . Brockner feels we need to have a chat about you. Evidently you were sick in school or something? There was talk about calling a doctor?"

Mom's voice had risen, and I shot an accusing glare at Deena. "Just a misunderstanding, Mom," I said quietly. The last thing I needed was for anyone to overhear us. "I'm fine."

Skirts billowed as she settled down on the grass beside us. Kill me. Just kill me now, I pleaded silently. I could see Brandi and Sara on the other side of the quad, the good side of the quad where the grass is still alive, staring at Mom. Tiffani walked across the parking lot, edged her way past us and craned her neck to get a better look as she crossed to where Brandi sat. Their boyfriends had gathered nearby, hackey sacks and other boy-crap forgotten as they got a good look at the three of us. Talk about your nightmares.

Mom tossed strands of long red hair back over one shoulder and beamed at Deena. "You and I have something in common," she said.

Oh, great, the one and only almost-friend I'd been able to get my hands on. "She means you both have long hair," I interjected quickly. "Long hair. And you like books. Right, Deena? You like books, right? Well, so does Mom. Right, Mom?"

They were staring at me in tandem and I babbled on. "So, listen Mom, maybe you should be getting in there. Getting in to see Mrs. Brockner. You had an appointment, right? She hates being kept waiting. Honestly. Drives her nuts. Not that I've ever kept her waiting, but this is what I hear."

"So, Deena." Mom had turned away from me with a shake of her head. "Has Ari told you what I do for a living?"

"No." Deena was grinning broadly at Mom, her features so altered by her smile I hardly recognized her. I'd never seen her look like that. She was really pretty. Normally she's extremely solemn and almost invisible – timid and quiet, like she's at a funeral.

"Mom's a house person," I said quickly. "You know, works around the house, does stuff with Dad. He's an artist."

Which was stretching things a bit, I'll admit, but calling Dad an artist was better than mentioning his origami flamingos, and it took the attention away from Mom and her psychic oddities. Desperation can make liars of us all.

"I'm a psychic," Mom said, and I clapped a hand to my forehead. "I pass on messages from the other side to assist people in living their best lives now."

"Really!" Deena grinned at Mom.

She looked positively elated, and once again I wondered just who and what she was. She didn't fit any neat little school slots. She was weird and odd, but she didn't seem to care what anyone thought. She studied like a maniac and yet she didn't really compete with the standard brainiacs, either. She stood on her own.

"How does that work?" she asked.

"And I've been expecting to meet you for some time now." Mom continued without answering, plowing her own path as usual. "I'm told you also have powers. I'm not entirely clear on what they are, but my feelings are you have been searching . . ."

"Look," I interrupted, "Mrs. Brockner awaits, Mom. Let's not forget you got a call from my school today. A call that totally freaked you out. A call that made you fear for my health. Let's not forget medical intervention was mentioned."

Damage control. It was all I could think about. Get her to stop talking and get her out of here.

"Come on now," I urged. "Up you get! Off you go!"

"What do the messages sound like?" Deena asked, and I groaned aloud. "Is it like hearing actual voices?"

"No." Mom was thoughtful. "More like thoughts. Not even really thoughts. More like just things you know without knowing how you know them."

Oh, yeah, like that makes perfect sense. I think I may have spoken my thoughts aloud, because Mom sighed heavily and turned to me.

"Ari, please," she said. "This terminal sarcasm you're struggling with has got to stop sometime. It's so negative. Be open to the forces around you. Every person's life is their own little script" – she waved her hands in the air – "and yours is only as strong as you make it. Smothering yourself in this sarcastic attitude is slowing your spiritual growth."

Well, her comment hurt, and I hate to admit how much, but my terminal sarcasm, as she called it, was the only thing that had kept me sane so far in my insane life. It was while I was informing her of this that I lost focus and forgot we were the centre of attention for the entire school, minus the girls' volleyball team, which practises during lunchtime. It was only when Sara's voice broke into my rant that I looked away from Mom.

We were the centre of attention, all right, just as I'd imagined in my most horrifying nightmares. Sara and Brandi were standing beside Deena, their mascaraed eyes wide, lip-glossed mouths half-open, and gathered around them were the boys who follow them everywhere they go.

"Is this your Mom?" Sara asked.

For once I was speechless and could only nod.

"Hi." She reached a hand out and Mom shook it. "I'm Sara."

"How do you do?"

"Um," she paused and then said in a rush, "did I hear Ari saying something about you talking to ghosts?"

Mom gave me an appraising look, and my face, which was already warm, became hotter. Even my hair was blushing.

"Yes," Mom answered, "although saying I talk to ghosts is really too simple." She was determined to elaborate on her chosen career. "It's much more complicated than that. But yes, sometimes I communicate with ghosts."

"Can you see the future?" Brandi's question came out in a rush.

"Sometimes I'm aware of upcoming events, or shown what might happen if certain choices are made." Mom was enigmatic as usual. "There are energies around all of us, and I am often shown how certain energies might be slowing or helping your progress in this life. Sometimes I see your other lives around you and that helps, too.

"And there are colours that show themselves around your body and through your aura that explain a lot about your physical and spiritual health," she mused, rambling on and on, in her own little world. It was hopeless trying to stop her once she got going. "Also, there are different pathways for you to take and many choices to make in this life you're living, and sometimes I can help with that."

Sara elbowed her way in past Deena, nearly stepping on her lunch in the process, and said in an awkward whisper, "Sometimes I feel like there's someone standing right behind me."

Mom nodded sagely. "There is," she said simply, and all I could do was sit there helplessly while Sara carried on in that same stage whisper.

"Can you help me find out who it is?"

I'm so bad at all this stuff; all the fitting in that everyone else seems to just pick up naturally is like deciphering a foreign language to me, one where you've been given a couple of vowels and maybe a consonant or two and the rest you have to figure out yourself. Any normal person would have seen an opportunity in Sara's interest. I saw her interest as a threat, a threat to any peaceful existence for me at school. A threat to ever belonging anywhere, anytime with anyone.

"Mom, please!" I was nearly begging, and at last she got the message.

"Yes." She turned her eyes to me finally. "Ariadne's right. I do have an appointment and shouldn't keep her waiting any longer."

She rose to her feet. "Goodbye girls, it was a pleasure meeting you," she said, and as she left she tossed out, "Maybe you can come visit Ari sometime."

The last I saw of her, as the crowd around me thinned out and returned to their pre-Mom activities, was of her bracelets catching the sun when she turned and waved before entering the school.

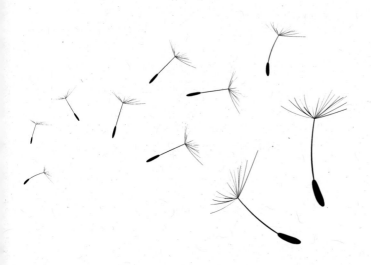

Chapter Twelve

"Mom, you need to understand that eventually everything – the whole complex world and everything in it – boils down to one very simple, very elementary formula." It was Friday night, a couple of days after her appearance at my school, and our conversation had hit one of those dead ends we've both become accustomed to. I paused to let my words sink in. This wasn't going to be easy for her, I realized that, but some things just have to be said. Sometimes a person has to be cruel in order to be kind. This was one of those times.

"Sex," I stated quietly, and paused for emphasis. "Procreation. Making carbon copies of each other. It's basic to all human and animal and plant activity. You really should know that by now."

I was working hard at helping her understand where exactly I was coming from. She was still obsessing about why I would allow, even encourage, someone whom she kept referring to as a previously unknown stock boy to cut my hair, and she was even more confused as to why I kept sighing over him. The fact I was rapidly becoming a woman and the fact this process had been speeded up by my meeting Eric was evidently too mind-boggling for her to take in.

Personally I could feel myself maturing like crazy these days, and I was a little surprised and disappointed she hadn't noticed.

"Don't you think there's someone at school you might like?" she asked. "Someone closer to your age? Maybe somebody in one of your classes. It would be nice to meet some of your friends, and if you were interested in a boy from school, then we could get to know his parents."

As usual, she was grabbing the ball and running with it and not listening to me. The very idea of my parents meeting other people's parents was the kind of thing to give me nightmares. One of the most attractive features of both Deena and Eric was their apparent lack of parental affiliates.

We were sitting at the kitchen table, me with a bowl of chocolate soy ice cream intended to soothe the realization that here I was again on a weekend night with no prospects other than the bowl in front of me. Mom sat opposite me with her chin propped on both hands and a look of concern on her face.

"Then you could go to movies with him and some other friends," she continued, totally not realizing I'd first have to make sure he wasn't some idiot who was going to spike my drink with some freaky drug. "And stop by to chat afterwards. I'd love to meet your friends."

Living in the past as she does, wandering around in her own little world, she was recalling a time from her own youth when all kids did was hang out at the local malt shop and hold hands. She wasn't even aware I'd have to be clear on which group of people he belonged to, so I'd know all the various diplomatic requirements, and that could take months, since sometimes the lines blur a little.

There is a whole whack of groups in my school. The brainiacs, the druggies, the jocks, the teacher faves, the completely scary and the physically attractive, to name a few. Nobody crosses lines. It's like the UN that way; you stay with the group that speaks your language. I didn't at the moment belong to any group, which was a lonely kind of feeling. Or maybe I *was* in a group – the loner group, the out of it, un-belonging group. I belonged, I suddenly realized, to the group of the people who don't belong in any group. Just thinking about it made my head hurt.

I returned to my original premise. "Mom, it matters not about guides, ambitions, good, bad, evil, harmony among nations . . ."

I paused and for a long moment I simply sat, my eyes fixed on hers with a kind of penetrating solemnity. Pulling her forcibly into my wavelength, sharing with her my view of the world. What I had to say was something I'd been putting off for a long time, although I'd been confident the day would eventually arrive when she'd be ready to hear me.

"Since at heart," I continued, "at the deepest, most intense core of the matter, every single thing everyone in the world does, from putting out forest fires to dusting bookshelves, all – *all* – is based on sheer animal lust."

I paused to gather breath and to let her absorb some of the shock. I realized it wasn't going to be easy for her to take the concept in. She likes to think I'm wrapped in a quilt and stowed in a closet somewhere out of the normal realm of things where I'll stay innocent and naïve all my life. It was time for her to see I'm actually a woman, and that as a woman I was totally drooling over Eric.

"Because, and Mom I cannot emphasize this enough, the whole world revolves around sex. Sex and only sex."

When she remained silent, I prompted, helpfully, "You remember sex? That innate drive you and Dad must have experienced at one point?"

I couldn't prevent a shudder, but I soldiered on. "The drive, the instinct to reproduce," I said, "that pulls between male and female of our species. Or" – I was so wrapped up in my subject I hardly knew what I was saying anymore – "between men and men sometimes, or women and women, except of course they don't actually have babies after it. And between dogs, parrots, bats, the mighty manatee . . ." I caught myself wandering from my intended path and scrambled back.

"Sex," I continued, "is the main gear the entire world turns on. The engine, if you will, upon which all else depends. Which brings me to my feelings for Eric."

I was hitting my stride now and could quite conceivably have gone on for hours, and maybe she sensed this because Mom broke in.

"Ariadne, please raise your mind up out of the gutter," she snapped, "and start placing more value on your guides and the role they play in your life. There is more to life than flirting with boys or daydreaming about romance."

"If my guides were half as helpful as they're cracked up to be," I returned, "they'd be telling me what I need to do to get Eric interested in me."

Other than hanging around the drugstore, I might have added, faking a casual interest in varieties of beauty aids that I had no intention of actually purchasing.

"Instead of wasting my time, out there in the ether some-where," I said instead and waved an arm impatiently, "hanging around meditating all the time!"

Poor Mom. Even I felt sorry for her as she sat there, seem-ingly stunned by my outburst. It didn't even bear thinking what Dad was going to say when he heard her version of the conversation. He's easily shocked. Easily intimidated. Kind of a throwback version of the hippie – love and peace and all that stuff. Anything that even hints at animosity throws him into a sort of panic.

"Sorry, Mom," I mumbled.

"It's OK." To my surprise, she wasn't loudly upset; in fact she was nearly whispering. There appeared to be tears in her eyes. "I'm so thrilled, Ariadne," she continued. "Sorry . . . Ari . . ." She smiled tremulously and sniffled. For once I was caught unpre-pared. Words actually failed me.

"I'm so pleased to hear you finally open up and acknowledge your guides' existence. You have no idea. I've waited so long for this! I'm so grateful to the universe!"

She'd missed the point entirely, which should have come as no surprise really, and I lifted a spoon thoughtfully to my mouth, thinking that I really should toss a few more chocolate chips into the remnants of ice cream, maybe a maraschino cherry or two as well. I was only half-listening as she continued.

"You realize, of course, that as you begin to follow your guides' direction and acknowledge the messages they send you, your life will change completely!"

Her excitement was obvious. And misplaced, but this wasn't the time to set her straight.

"Colours will be so vibrant! The sky will seem huge! Stars will be brighter. You'll feel like you finally belong in your skin, and you'll never look back! All the things you do will have more meaning and more strength to them. You will become a beacon to others. Someone they can trust and follow and believe in."

Beacon? Not exactly what I'd had in mind. I'd been thinking more along the lines of becoming a sort of born-again sex symbol. Someone with a kind of jazzy energy around her – a hint of danger, a dash of adventure, an animal magnetism. In my mind was a picture of myself altered, the old Ari replaced by a goddess.

The hairdo, which was already beginning to lose its initial appeal, would have grown out into amber waves bouncing along my shoulders. My willowy figure would be clothed in a cool pair of low-cut jeans. The hint of my tattoo (which of course I didn't actually have yet), a Celtic symbol twining its way along the base of my spine, would be just barely visible as my skinny little shirt rode up a bit in the back.

". . . so they'll be here tomorrow evening," Mom was saying, "around seven or so, and I thought maybe you'd like to plan the menu with me."

The mental image I'd lovingly conjured up of myself faded fast as I tuned back in. "What?" I said. "What's that again?"

Mom sighed in frustration, and then a sudden thought made her beam with delight. "I knew you weren't listening to me," she said, and added coyly, "but tuning in to your guides is much more important."

She threw her arms around my neck and hugged me across the table. "Ariadne, I'm just so thrilled for you!"

OK. Thrilled, yes, but what exactly was all that stuff about menus? "OK, Mom," I soothed, as I disentangled myself. "But what's this menu business about? Is grandma coming over?"

And then a new thought made me groan aloud. "It's not another one of those psychic gatherings full of drama queens again, is it?" My voice had risen and I brought it back to a less abrasive level. "Because if you're planning on filling the house with nutcases again, Mom, I'm not . . . "

"Ariadne! They are not 'nutcases'!" Our momentary truce seemed to be over. "And I resent you calling my clients by that demeaning name."

OK, fine. I rolled my eyes, but remained silent.

"The people who come for my readings," she said forcefully, "are people who have opened their spiritual eyes to the vast unseen realms surrounding us. They need help; they need someone to listen and to support them. They are not crazy in any sense of the word!"

"Sorry," I mumbled.

She sat there, still steaming for a moment, and as I watched she slowly breathed in three long inhalations and then whooshed them out again. Cleansing breaths she calls them, and claims they clear the negative stuff from around her. She does this quite often.

"These girls seemed perfectly nice to me," she said finally, when she dropped back to earth, "and they're obviously interested in expanding their consciousness, so when they arrive I expect you to treat them with respect."

"What girls?" I asked reasonably.

"Sara is one of them," she answered, "and I think the other one has some sort of strange name as well as a very confusing aura . . ."

"Brandi?" I was aghast. "Brandi and Sara are coming over? Over here?"

"Good heavens," she huffed, "what's wrong with that? Of course they're coming here. I can't do readings at your school, can I? Well, actually, I guess I could," she said, answering her own rhetorical question, "but the atmosphere here is much more conducive to an accurate reading."

She glanced around the kitchen and I followed her gaze, seeing the room suddenly through the eyes of the two most prominent members of the G6.

An incense stick sizzled hazily in a handmade ceramic Celtic-cross tray, sending the sweetly smoky scent of rosemary through the air. A large blue and grey dreamcatcher drooped over the kitchen table, a leftover relic from Kenny's mom, our long-ago neighbour from way back, whose Granddad had been a shaman. She'd evidently been aware of some of the weird goings-on happening at our place and decided we needed all the help we could get. Two of its long, dangling feathers had been slightly mangled by Tonto, our ancient resident housecat, but that was really the least of my concerns.

The kitchen chairs, a group of mismatched garage sale finds that were swathed in brilliant green and gold sari fabric to hide their disreputable appearance, were so broken down they wiggled tipsily when sat on. The sari fabric at least offered protection from splinters, but anyone sitting in them had to be prepared to brace with whatever limbs they had available, to prevent toppling over onto our worn and faded linoleum.

But it was Mom's eclectic and unconventional group of risqué cat figurines that worried me most. The collection was all Dad's fault. It had started one year when he'd forgotten her birthday for about the third time in a row. Even Dad, innocent child that he can be, knew he was in deep trouble. His desperation led to one of his more insane decisions when he found what he thought of as a 'cute ceramic kitty' at a local flea market. The man was so naïve he didn't even see what that kitty was up to. It was the start of a long chain of odd decorative cats in assorted shapes and sizes that have graced our lives since and which Mom seems to treasure and I prefer to not dwell on. They live in the kitchen, on top of cabinets, behind the drainer rack, next to the toaster.

And then there was the ceiling to think about.

Dad had become obsessed over the last month with birds, and not just any birds, but cranes in particular, a fairly narrow subject it would seem to any normal person not obsessed with the topic. It had begun on the day he picked up an old *National Geographic* at the library that featured an article on Japan and birds of the Far East. He rapidly become so obsessed with cranes and their mystical qualities that he'd insisted on reading parts of the accompanying article out loud at dinner, his voice lingering in a loving way on any sentence with the word 'crane' in it. It was like he'd found a spiritual home for himself.

Now every square inch of ceiling featured a thumbtacked dangling origami crane. He'd folded them from a variety of wallpapers and made them in different sizes and colours to represent adults and chicks. He'd even folded some egg-shaped forms: the un-born. They hung over our heads, drifting lazily along with every breeze, their wings and beaks pointing in odd directions. His intended goal was to infest our house with a thousand origami cranes in a misguided attempt to cash in on the premise that a batch of cranes that size were somehow holy or magical and had the power to grant wishes. Of course, he never stated what his wish might be, obviously, since that would no doubt screw up the whole process, kind of like the superstition about blowing out birthday candles and probably, knowing Dad as I do, it's better not to ask. Ignorance can indeed be bliss, but it doesn't alter the fact that whenever anyone walked through the kitchen a small tidal wave of cranes fluttered in their wake.

"We'll be in the living room, right?" I asked. "I mean, we'll have to discuss the menu as you mentioned, but we'll actually have the food and the readings in the living room?"

"And I want you to ask Deena to come as well," Mom said, sidestepping my kitchen concerns, "because there are things she needs to hear."

"Mom, Deena's not really my friend, but she's the closest thing I have to one and I really don't know if . . ."

"Deena needs to be here," Mom stated firmly. "This is happening because of her. Her presence is crucial."

"Why? Why is her presence so crucial? What if she can't come?"

"She will come."

I hate it when she gets like this. "Mom," I tried again, "Deena is a busy girl. She has all these older cool friends to hang around with. I'm not sure she'll be able to be here."

Mentioning those older friends of Deena's brought Eric's face to mind, and once again I vowed to make sure that even after I was a fully accepted member of the G6 themselves, I'd shove Deena through that hallowed doorway as well. Although, she seemed not only less than impressed by the G6, but also actually slightly repulsed by them. This reaction, I reasoned, was probably based on her belief she'd never fit in. I intended to prove her wrong. Whether she liked it or not.

"Mom," I said, "I'm not even sure how to get hold of her. I only see her at school."

"Go see that friend of hers." Mom grabbed my empty bowl and placed it in the sink. "The one at the drugstore. I'm sure he has her phone number.

"Just remember, Ariadne, she should be here tomorrow night at seven o'clock." Her voice drifted away down the hall.

"But *why* is it all happening because of her?" I objected loudly, attempting to appeal to Mom's reasonable side, which of course, she doesn't have. "Why do we have to subject Deena to all this junk?"

"Call her," she replied vaguely, disappearing into the nether regions.

It was useless arguing with her, and as she shut the door to her room, I found myself sitting staring blankly at the kitchen table and wondering how my life could possibly get any more ridiculously screwed up.

Chapter Thirteen

Facebook: Between you and M. Collins
02-21-Yearofourlordwhatever

OK, so I realize you've ended the Facebook experiment and I know it's Saturday and we don't have school, but I can't seem to help myself. Evidently someone's parental unit complained about privacy issues and you've had to abort. It wasn't my parental unit though, since neither of them have a clue, and so do you mind if I continue?

You don't have to read these things or respond or anything, but it tends to ease my mind to write this stuff down and send it out there. Just saying. Not that I can't cope without writing this stuff down, but it helps to clear my head up a little bit when I do write it down. Not a lot. But some.

OK, 'nuff said. Just so you know that this does help and I am grateful if you don't mind me filling up your Facebook box with my messy life. Like I said, you can just ignore it. Or delete. There's a little box on top that says 'delete.' You can just click on that once you have the little pointy arrow on it. K?

I explained to my mother about sex last night. She's so far out there in her own little planetary system of entities, auras and voices from the beyond that she doesn't see me as a real person! A sexual person. A woman. She only sees me as her offspring, her kid, a child, not as an actual person with real feelings. She can't understand how I don't want to live her kind of life. She refuses to see how I want to live my own life, by my own standards, with my own interests and beliefs. She doesn't realize my life is based on the real stuff around me and sexual attraction is becoming a part of that.

And she really doesn't understand how I have fallen crazy in love with a guy I only met because of Deena. He's the one who cut my hair, in case you weren't aware. He's so talented. And very cute. Long dark brown hair in a ponytail, brown eyes and a little beard and he's got a relaxed, funny way about him. But she refuses to think of me growing up and not being her little girl anymore.

And furthermore, she's horning her way into my social life here at school by inviting Sara and Brandi and who knows who else over to our house for a psychic reading! OMG!! This sucks. This sucks big-time.

There's no use arguing with her either, because as soon as anyone tries talking sense, and I mean anyone, including dad, she gets all dopey and dreamy and wanders away in mid-sentence.

Or else she starts describing some previous life in an old hut or along a lake she can't remember the name of. Or she re-enacts, in tedious detail, a conversation she had with someone nobody has ever met or heard of but which she insists happened that afternoon in an undisclosed location while she was meditating. It's aggravating.

Her favorite tactic with me is to go into great detail about a life she evidently lived in India or someplace (all she knows is she sees a hot sun and flimsy little shacks with crowds of dark-eyed kids around and plenty of dust), where I was the boy who lived down the alley and I had a million different

He cast an appraising glance

talents in the psychic sphere and she was so enraptured by me that she swore in her next life (this one, obviously) she'd have talents like mine and be all clairvoyant and spiritual to impress this boy (who is now me, according to her) and all I can say is what a pile of absolute crap!

There. That felt pretty good.

Thanks for listening/reading/deleting/whatever. TTYL.

The question I'd asked myself at the table with Mom on Friday night about how my life could possibly get worse was answered for me next morning as I stood in the drugstore attempting nonchalance and staring into the deep purple-brown of Eric's eyes.

I'd done my best to derail Mom's plans, but all to no avail. It was her insistence on coming with me if I needed help that had finally propelled me out the door. None of it seemed to matter anymore anyway, since Eric was proving to be a tough guy to start a conversation with.

"So," I continued awkwardly, "if you have Deena's phone number I'd really appreciate it and then I can call her and . . ."

"Who are you?"

"I'm Ari," I explained patiently. Again. We'd already been through this once, but he seemed to have an extremely short memory. "Deena's friend? Remember? You did my hair?"

"Oh, yeah." His voice was a slow drawl. "I kinda thought I knew you from somewhere. Yeah. The hair."

He cast an appraising glance at my head where the little pentagon shapes were already blurring as the shaved lines grew back in.

"Needs a trim," he offered.

"Yes, well," I cleared my throat, "I thought I'd let it grow for a while. You know."

"Yeah, that'd be good. It's kinda weird lookin'." He lifted one hand and brushed the top of my head. "Still feels nice and bristly, though."

"Yes, well." My mouth was so dry I could barely speak. "Thank you."

Thank you for touching me, my mind cried, thank you for being so cute, thank you for being born a boy.

"So," I said after another long, uncomfortable silence, "do you have her number?"

It seemed somewhat crude to drag the conversation back to its original topic, but it had to be done and, besides, I couldn't think of anything else to say.

"You know," I prompted, "for Deena?" He was so very cute, but at the same time I was beginning to realize he possessed a certain exasperatingly vague quality lurking beneath the surface.

"Deena. Yeah." He nodded slowly. "No, I don't have her number." And as my heart sank, he added, "But I know where she's living. Saw her going in one day."

"You do? You did? Can you tell me how to get there?" By now there was a certain obsessive quality to the whole experience and I'd become so wrapped up in getting through the fog surrounding him, I'd forgotten my initial shyness. "Or show me?"

"Show you? Yeah, I can show you. That'd be better. I'm not too good at giving directions."

Somehow this didn't surprise me. "OK," I said.

By that point I'd have agreed to nearly anything. His vagueness and the absent-minded qualities that might have annoyed another, or actually driven some people to openly violent acts, only endeared him to me more. It's true, I thought with a certain pleased triumph, love is completely blind and accepting.

At the same time, however, I was pretty confident that I'd be able to change some of his more irritating habits eventually. Of course it would take time, but I can be patient if I need to be, all other appearances to the contrary. I realized any such changes would have to wait until he was so wildly in love with me that he'd be willing to do anything to keep me. That scenario played itself out in a pleasant, never-ending spiral through my imagination as I stood there waiting patiently in the shampoo aisle for him to come back from talking to his supervisor.

I have to admit, even in my most optimistic moments, the thought of Deena and Eric and whatever had transpired between them the night I got my hair cut still lurked, seething at the back of my mind, ticking away like a crazy little alarm clock. I had no real idea what kind of relationship they had going between them, and the part of me that's a jealous maniac got busy working its destructive magic every time I allowed it to enter my thoughts, but being there on his turf – the place where we'd first met – seemed to open the door to a variety of other scenarios.

Absently, I nudged a couple of shampoo bottles into tighter alignment and stood back to admire the effect. It would be kind of cool to stock shelves, I thought suddenly, working hand-in-hand so to speak, with Eric. Becoming his assistant, his right-hand man as it were, the person he'd look forward to seeing every day, someone he'd come to view as his closest confidante, and *not*, definitely not, a sister or only a friend.

Indulging in a brief fit of fantasy, I could see myself looking kind of cute in that dark-blue aprony thing the drugstore makes its staff wear. Paired up with a really great pair of tight jeans and with the edges of some sweet little top teasing around the neckline, even the apron could have its flattering qualities.

Of course, as a staff member who dresses well and whose killer heels are not really meant for actual work, I'd undoubtedly have some slight difficulty in lifting one of the heavier boxes, which in turn would give Eric an opportunity to behave in a manly fashion and come to my aid. Which in turn would give us a chance to laugh lightly together at how strong he was. It would become sort of a running joke with us, so that he'd basically do all the heavy lifting after that, leaving me free to admire the muscles moving under the back of his T-shirt as he shifted boxes all over the place.

I could see myself perched seductively on a stool in the back room, where it would be kind of dark and no doubt a little bit scary with only a couple of narrow shafts of light beaming through the dusty air. I'd be sitting, the end of a pen propped reflectively in my mouth, teasing the corners of my lips, unaware that Eric was watching me while I filled out long, involved order forms.

His admiration would grow daily, as I deciphered some crazy order that had been completely screwed up at the place where they manufacture all the shampoos and so forth (a place I somehow envisioned as being a big white building filled with bubbles), thus saving him endless hours of painstaking paperwork. Being a man of action, not words, he'd find himself filled with gratitude and a sense of awe at my competence.

I'd become indispensable to him, and then in some blinding flash, as a beam of sunlight lit up the highlights in my hair and I continued to solve his problems for him, totally unaware that he was constantly studying my every move, he'd suddenly reach out and grab me in a warm embrace, pulling me roughly off my stool, his lips searching for mine, the heat from his body penetrating those aprony things we both were forced to wear.

A long sigh burst from me, and through the haze of my fantasies I watched Eric walk toward me, his jeans low on his hips and a pleasantly distracted expression on his face.

"Hey," he said companionably, "let's go. I gotta talk to Deena about my elbow."

ChapterFourteen

"**W**hat do you mean, you asked him to show you!" Deena was outraged. She stood there holding the screen door in her hand, blocking my view of the house interior.

"Deena, c'mon," I pleaded. "Mom says you've gotta be there, and she's already got Brandi and Sara coming over! It's a nightmare! It's just horrible." There was a sob at the back of my voice, and it wasn't only because she was so unwelcoming.

The whole day had taken on a 'maybe I should just run away from home' quality, and Eric's presence on the way to Deena's hadn't helped. He'd treated me like a little kid, not the hot chick I'd hoped he'd see. He'd started by asking me what my favourite school subject was and stopped just short of ruffling my hair and asking which I liked better, grape or orange Popsicles. The answer, of course, would be grape, but it was still insulting.

"You have to help me," I said. "Please."

"I don't know." She glanced behind her. "This isn't a good time, Ari. I mean, maybe I'll come over sometime, but . . ."

"No, no, no, you have to promise me!" There was an insistent voice at the back of my head warning me of possible total disaster if I didn't have some sort of backup tonight. Deena may not seem terribly impressed by any of the G6 but, on the other hand, unlike myself, she's not intimidated by them either.

"Hey, c'mon," Eric put in. He was hovering behind me, craning around to see inside the house Deena was guarding. "Give the kid a break, Deena."

I gritted my teeth. "Yeah," I said, "give me a break. Please!" I hate to beg anyone for anything, but in this case I was willing to compromise my principles. "Deena, I need you."

As she continued to shake her head, I said in a rush, "Mom's doing a reading for these guys tonight! I've never watched her do this stuff before! Usually she's got a bunch of crazy ladies in there with her and I just avoid everyone and hang out in my room, or sometimes with dad out in the garage, but tonight this is the first time she's doing her thing with people I actually know, and she says I have to be there and . . ."

"Fine!" she snapped, and when a voice inside the house called her name, she added quickly, "I'll be there tonight."

Eric lifted his elbow and opened his mouth to speak and she said, "Go away, Eric. I'll come over later. You" – she glared at me – "you better come in."

"My elbow," Eric started.

"Stop it!" Deena ordered.

"Who's in there?" he asked, trying to peer past her. "Who you living with?"

"Nobody. None of your business," she said.

"Hey, you're talking to me. Eric," he stated, and thumped his chest to drive the point home. "Your old partner in crime. Remember?"

Things were starting to get interesting. I leaned against the porch railing and tried to disappear so they wouldn't realize I was all ears. Not literally, of course, but figuratively. I was just curious, that's all. My ears are a normal size.

"Remember that pregnant lady?"

Deena threw a glance at me and started to shush him.

"Remember how she threw us out? Man, that was tough. Where'd you go anyway? One minute you were right there and the next minute you were gone." He sounded annoyed. "Man, me and Carl, we looked for you everywhere."

"Carl and I," I corrected automatically and then slapped my hand over my mouth.

"Eric, I swear," she started, and even he began to hear the threat in her voice. "If you don't get out of here right now, I will personally . . ."

"OK." He held his hands up in surrender. "OK, you come over whenever you want. Just cool it. My elbow's not going anywhere." Eric backed away, hands still raised. "See ya later, Ari."

A woman standing near the stove waved a spatula at me as Deena pulled me through the door. "Ari, this is Mel. Mel is my auntie." She spoke as though the words were being forced out of her.

"Hi," I said.

"You're Ari? The kid from school?" Mel asked. "Deena's mentioned you." And I thought I saw her hide a smile before she turned back to her frying pan. "Want a grilled cheese?"

"Sure."

"Pickles?"

"Absolutely."

She turned and grinned at me when I answered. The grooves on either side of her mouth deepened and I smiled back, liking how her eyes lit up with humour.

"In the fridge," she said, motioning with her spatula. "Top shelf. Deena put an extra plate out, please. Ari, grab a knife and slice a few of those pickles into a bowl. The chips are on the counter and you guys can put out some glasses for juice."

When Mom cooks it's usually a sort of tense and sometimes dangerous situation. She's so easily distracted and the smoke alarm is so touchy that we often seem to be preparing food in the middle of some kind of homemade catastrophe. This was different. Relaxing.

There was something very calming about Mel and the way she moved quietly around her kitchen, putting sandwiches in front of Deena and me and telling me I was welcome when I thanked her for the food. She was simply just a really nice woman, so easygoing that it felt almost as if I'd met her before, although it could have been just her resemblance to Deena that made me feel that way. It seemed totally normal, almost like coming home again, to grab a chair and sit down while she put the food in front of us, sat down across from me and passed the chips my way.

Mel was tall and thin with dark hair and eyes that resembled Deena's. She whistled tunelessly between her teeth while she flipped another helping of grilled cheese sandwiches. It was hard to pinpoint why exactly, but she seemed content and independent, standing there at the stove in torn, faded jeans and a red tee. She didn't talk much, which was a nice change after the non-stop racket I was used to in my own home, and she projected an attitude that made it seem as if she'd be totally OK if everyone else on earth simply disappeared. It's an attitude that Deena often seems to share and which makes me a little crazy with envy. I'd love to be that free. It'd be nice to not always compare myself to other people, mostly because when I do the comparing, I always end up losing. I'm never as cute or as smart or as friendly or funny, or just as good as I want to be. I'm always lacking something. It's annoying.

Mel's long graying hair was pulled back from her face in a ponytail held by a coloured elastic. In a way she seemed ageless, even though she was probably pretty old, judging by the lines on her face. They were most defined when she smiled, and when she laughed aloud, as she did when I sighed to Deena about Eric being too blind to see the real me, the lines made brackets around her eyes and mouth.

The fact I'd been welcomed into the place I'd envisioned as Deena's pod was a little intimidating, but at the same time energizing. It felt good there. I felt welcome. And the sand-wiches were good, too. It was easy to sit there and talk and eat pickles and grilled cheese and watch Deena and her aunt be ordinary people together.

"Thanks for the lunch." I took my plate to the sink and then sat back down.

We'd finished eating and I wasn't sure what my role here was or what I was expected to do next, but the sandwiches were gone and Mel was watching me from across the little Arborite table like I reminded her of an interesting but slightly gross science experiment. It was nice to be the centre of atten-tion. I liked it, which in turn meant I had no intention of letting it end any time soon.

"This is a nice house." By which I meant it was completely unlike my own home. There were precisely zero paper cranes flapping over the table, for example.

"You should see my place," I rattled on, in attempt to not have to go home and face the upcoming disastrous evening. "Well, I guess you will tonight, Deena, and thanks for coming over, but I've got to warn you it is freaky. But you might like it, and since you've already met Mom your expectations can't be that high."

I paused, and since both Deena and her aunt continued to just sit there silently I kept talking. Silence might be 'golden' and all that, but mostly it makes me nervous, and besides, I honestly love to talk. Not too many people are that willing to listen, and there was no way I'd walk away and ignore a great opportunity like this. A captive audience, so to speak.

"I wish I lived with my aunt instead of just my parents," I mused conversationally. "Or at least someone not directly related and someone who could see me as an individual and not just their 'kid.' I am more than just a kid," I added warmly. "I do have a life of my own, and some people are gonna have to realize that at some point!"

"Oops, Ari. Be careful what you wish for," Mel said. "Some people would give a lot for an ordinary family."

"Yeah," I said, "true, but I bet you guys have so much more fun together. Ordinary families are" – I paused and searched for the right word – "ordinary," I finished, "and I bet you guys have way more laughs and understand each other way more than my Mom and me."

Deena shook her head at me. "Family is what you make it," she stated, and it was obvious she wasn't interested in any opinions to the contrary or any complaints from me. "I think we can choose our family if we want, just like we choose our friends.

"You are the only family I need," she said to Mel in a tone that left no room for argument or comment. She turned to me. "When I found that Metis drop-in centre downtown, for the first time I could remember, I felt like there was a community of people who look like me, where I could belong. The foster places were all white. I felt 'wrong' in them, and I really missed being part of a real family."

"OK," I said, somehow unable to stop myself from yammering on, "so the foster places were awful, which believe me, I can honestly understand, because life with mom and dad can be pretty horrifying at times, but you must have parents around somewhere, so I'm sure you understand what a pain they can be."

Even as the words left my mouth, I realized it probably wasn't the best idea to head in this direction, because really who knew what godawful thing might have happened. I do read the news headlines once in a while, and so I'm not completely off the radar; I know terrible stuff happens. On the other hand, I've never been known as diplomatic, which in some eyes might be seen as a positive virtue. Of course, this lack of tact can also be seen as a real downer, and evidently that's how Deena interpreted it.

"My parents," she said coldly, "are none of your business." She stood from the table and looked pointedly at the back door.

"C'mon now," Mel said quietly. "Let's get along, ladies."

"Why are you here?" Deena didn't seem to be asking a simple question, so much as accusing me of intruding. "Why does a white girl like you suddenly want to be my best friend?"

I have to admit I was stunned for a second. Flabbergasted. Speechless. Not for long, obviously, since being speechless is like a foreign concept to me, but still it kept me quiet for a second or two. I'd honestly never thought of myself as a 'white girl' before, and in my mind I saw a ghostly figure wrapped in a sheet, ghastly pale and wan. That wasn't what Deena meant, I realized, but that's what the phrase conjured up.

In the same, rather doltish way, I'd never thought of Deena as anything but Deena, although I now realized she wasn't a 'white girl' at all. She was brown. Brownish. Aboriginal, obviously, since that detail had already been pointed out to me by Brandi, but which kind of Aboriginal was still up for debate. Kind of like saying your background is northern European, which only narrowed it down to mean you could be the offspring of Laplanders or a Danish duke. Meaning that genetically you could be totally into either herding reindeer, or manufacturing tiny houses out of plastic bricks.

Mel gave her a sharp look, but Deena was on a roll now. "Why are you suddenly turning up all over the place, borrowing stuff and insisting on hanging out together? Why are you so interested in me?"

"Who, me?"

Deena glared down at me. "Yes, you," she said flatly. "Why are you here?"

"To ask you to come over to my place tonight." It seemed pretty obvious to me. "Mom made me."

"Your mom 'made' you?" She snorted. "Your mom 'made' you?" Her voice rose. "I've met your mom, I like your mom, but your mom 'made' you!"

I hadn't realized how potentially insulting the truth might sound. "Well, not exactly 'made me,'" I amended quickly. "But it was a very strong suggestion."

Mel snorted a laugh and Deena made a disgusted sound, slammed her chair back under the table and turned and left the kitchen.

"Holy. Pretty rude," Mel observed after she'd gone. She leveled a long look at me. "You and Deena getting pretty close?"

"Sort of. I dunno. It's hard to make friends."

I was still a little shaken by Deena's comment about me being a 'white' girl. The phrase sort of glowed neon-bright in my head, and the impression stuck in my chest, like something lumpy I'd swallowed that wouldn't quite go down properly. I'd never been called that before, and the only thing I was absolutely sure of was that I was completely unsure what to think. It hurt a little.

Mel leaned back in her chair and waved as Deena strode back through the kitchen and yanked the back screen door open.

"Going to see Eric," she called as the door swung shut behind her. "Ari, go home. I'll see you tonight."

"You hang out together." Mel broke the silence that followed the slamming of the screen door. "You come over here today." Mel gave a half-smile. "C'mon, Ari, what's up?"

"Look," I began. There was a hint of a sob lurking, and I gave myself a shake and a moment to get my head together.

Suddenly I was so tired of carrying this mother-shaped burden around. Tired of being a loner and odd and out of it, tired of everything. Sharing with Mel seemed like it might ease my load. She looked trustworthy. Deena liked her obviously, and I trusted Deena, so why not. Why not share some of this crap and see what others think about it.

"Look," I continued, "my mother's a psychic. Or so she says. Personally I have my doubts. But tonight she's invited these really popular girls over. Girls from school. These are girls who can make my life a living hell if they want to and I need Deena there. And plus, Mom says she's gotta come."

"Why would your mom want Deena there so bad?"

"Because." I stopped short.

It was a little difficult to know how much I should confide in Mel, a person I'd just met, but then on the other hand I was in one of those 'what the hell' moods, and my moods often seem to rule me more than I'd like. Moods aside, at this point I was also beginning to feel a twinge of conscience and talking to Mel felt like it might ease some of the guilt beginning to build up inside. It was one thing to storm the ramparts of the G6 on my own and another to use Deena as a battering ram. Although by now I was aware that Deena not only wouldn't be any help, she'd be more likely to toss a grenade or two at me to prevent me from reaching what she, and no doubt Mel, would think was a pretty stupid and lame goal.

I decided to come clean. G6 be damned! More or less, anyway. Even I, blinded by ambition as I had been, was beginning to grow weary of the whole exercise and plus, I liked Mel. She was cool. Easy and nice.

"Mom says Deena has special gifts of some sort. I have no idea what they are, but Mom wants to help her," I blurted.

When Mel didn't respond, I added, "Mom's weird, I freely admit it. You won't get any arguments from me about that. I think she's crazy, but she's also totally dedicated to her spiritual stuff. She says it can be difficult sometimes, because regular people can get a little skittish, and she wants to support Deena. At least that's pretty much what she said last night. The parts I listened to, anyway.

"Personally," I added, "I think Mom wishes she had someone to share her interests, which I don't, and so that's why she keeps bugging me about it all."

Mel sighed and stood to fill the kettle. "Tea?" she offered.

The kitchen was sunny, clean, worn, a little shabby, and comfortable. I nodded. "Tea would be great," I said.

So Mel and I sat there, watched the tea steep and kept silent for what seemed like eons, but was really only time for both of us to catch our thoughts.

ChapterFifteen

The sun shone warm through white-framed windows and cast golden patterns on the Formica table. The table was an ancient, but pretty, many-shaded green with a wide chrome trim, and I was absently tracing a finger through the design when Mel spoke again.

"I think I know what your mom means about support. Deena and me are Metis. That can cause problems, too." She laughed. "People get 'skittish' about us, sometimes too."

Mel blew on her tea and gazed over the cup at me. Her look was speculative, as if this was a test of some sort. A test I might fail miserably. A situation I'm fairly familiar with. "Do you know what 'Metis' means?"

I offered a careful nod, a little unsure, but casting my mind back over previous social studies classes. Metis: Aboriginal people plus European people, mating like crazy all over the place equals Metis kids who become Metis adults who have more Metis kids. Not exactly the Wikipedia definition, but close enough I figured. I nodded again, this time more sure of myself.

"We are an in-between culture in many ways," Mel continued. "An in-between people and an in-between culture, but we are finding our voice. This has not been an easy life for Deena. She's careful. She was on the street, not for long, but long enough to learn to be careful.

"It hasn't been an easy life for me, either," she added and then went on. "But then sometimes the easy life is the least interesting. Sometimes difficulties in life are what give it sparkle and energy and intensity. But it can still be hard to handle."

This wasn't what I'd been expecting and it kind of threw me. What I'd been expecting was for Mel to start acting like most adults do around me: solicitous, over-caring, throwing around some smothering motherly stuff, kind of dorky. Instead, she was direct. She confided something. She treated me like a real person. It caught me off-guard, but I liked it.

"Deena's mother was my sister." Mel sent a long, straight and level look at me. "My little sister. She died many years ago. Drugs. And Deena's father" – here Mel seemed to fight a minor internal battle with herself – "was a jerk. He left Deena alone a lot after her mother died. His other kids, too. We don't know where they are anymore."

At this point, Mel stopped and stared out the window for a long moment.

"You take it easy with Deena," she said finally. "Your mom's right. I know Deena's got gifts. She's like her grandma that way. My mother. She was a healer – respected and sometimes feared. You've got some gifts yourself." She poured water over tea leaves and sat back down. "You two girls take it easy. Promise me."

"I promise."

"I don't want Deena hurt again, and I don't want a bunch of crazy little high school kids hanging around my house, either," she said shortly. "You get my drift?"

"Yup." I sipped at my tea and waited a minute. My throat was a little plugged up, and it took a swallow or two to loosen it so I could talk. "What do you mean, 'gifts?'"

"Whose?" she asked. "Deena's or yours? Or mine?" She laughed at my look. "No", she said to my unasked question, "I don't have any of those type gifts. But I do have the ability to spot them in others. And I'm talking psychic or intuitive gifts, no other kind. Don't know what other things you might be good at, but I do know what I see coming from you."

No. No, she didn't. Much as I liked Mel, there was no way I was buying into any of this 'gifts' business.

"I don't have any of those kinds of gifts," I stated firmly. "I have no talents. I'm zero in the supernatural department. Zilch. Zippo." On this one thing I was absolutely not backing down. "I don't have a belief system, and I don't want a belief system. I'm a non-believer and I like it that way."

Mel was watching me. Sipping her tea. Tracing a finger around the rim of her cup. Her calm was making me nervous and maybe I should have just shut up, but I couldn't seem to help myself.

"It's simple!" I said bluntly. "There's nothing out there. It's one big cosmic joke, all that spooky psychic stuff. Ghosts. Bodiless voices. Entities." I waved my hands in the air. "Auras! What a bunch of crap. I mean, what else can I believe?" I paused for a moment, and when Mel didn't reply I went on.

"If there's another dimension and guides and all this woo-woo stuff going on, then who the heck is in charge? Am I supposed to think that we're all in some stupid experiment? That somebody out there in the invisible sky is watching us like a sitcom gone bad and saying, 'Well, crap, maybe I need to do a rewrite? Maybe find a different leading man? How about a little leg, maybe if they show a little leg, this show'll be a hit?' Is that what I'm supposed to believe?

"If there are 'guides' and 'angels,' or whatever you want to call them, out there," I finished crabbily, "handing this stuff out like some sort of 'gift,' I want them to know I don't want it. I want no part of any of this stuff. There's no freaking way I want to be like my Mom."

It was a risky tactic telling Mel about Mom, but what made things OK was that Mel didn't seem to want to convert me the way Mom did. She let me vent. Mom would've flipped a gasket when I said I didn't believe in any of her mumbo-jumbo. Mel just let me disbelieve as much as I wanted.

Deena slammed the screen door open and stormed into the kitchen again at that point. Her entrance into the room jolted the atmosphere like a small and noisy cyclone, disturbing the air and making the little hairs on my arm tingle. I sat a little straighter, her 'white girl' remark still stinging slightly.

"You still here?" She pulled out her chair and sat.

"Want some tea?" Mel asked, and at Deena's nod she got up and grabbed another cup from the cupboard.

With Deena back in the house, it seemed pretty obvious to me this whole situation had become a lot more tricky. Things could go either way, either really good or really bad depending on what was said. So I decided, uncharacteristically, to say nothing at all. And besides, I'd already probably said too much.

"That was a quick trip," Mel observed. "Eric all better now?"

Deena sighed and gazed into her tea. "I'll see Eric later. I just went round the block for a little air."

"We were talking, me and Ari, about your mom and dad. And other things."

"I figured as much," Deena said. She half-smiled at her aunt. "Why do you think I decided I should be back here? Keep an eye on you two. Make sure the family secrets stay secret."

Both of them laughed and then looked over at me. Deena sighed.

"Look Ari," she said finally, "I realize you're a little young and maybe you're in over your head here, so if you'd like to just scram and go home, then please go and I'll see you at school next week."

"What about tonight?"

"I'll come over tonight if you want, but honestly this whole friendship thing that you seem so sure about is a little weird.

You've got to admit it's odd. We can just go back to seeing each other at school and leave it there."

At that point, I knew exactly what I wanted and it wasn't that. Hanging in the kitchen with Mel and Deena felt so good and so comfortable. It wasn't something weird or odd at all, it was just what friends do. Or at least, it's what I'd always anticipated friends would do. Who knew? Maybe this situation was completely off the radar, but at this point I was willing to take that chance.

"I'm not that young," I said indignantly. "Depending on how you look at it, I'm practically 17. Give or take," I added grudgingly.

"Give or take, what? A couple of years?" Mel laughed.

I shrugged. "More or less. But," I rushed on victorious, Mom's nutty logic finally coming in handy, "age is only a number."

Quoting Mom always gives me the heebie-jeebies, going against my better judgment as it usually does, but in this case it seemed to hit a nerve both in my case and in the case of those I was attempting to convince. It made a sort of twisted sense, which of course I was naturally reluctant to admit, but I carried on anyway. "Some people are old from the day they're born and some people are young when they're 90, so anatomical age doesn't count."

They looked at each other and both laughed aloud.

"My body is young, but my soul is old," I stated firmly. "And don't tell my mother I said that."

At Deena's look, I said, "Hey, you have your family secrets and I have mine."

Facebook: Between you and M. Collins
02-21-Yearofourlordwhatever

I realize Facebooking you twice in one day is a little extreme, but it's been an extreme kind of day.

I learned some stuff today. Not school stuff, obviously, and don't even ask about homework because it's not Sunday night, so no, I haven't started it yet. But, did you know Deena's Metis? And that she grew up in foster care places mostly? And were you aware she now lives with her aunt that she found through an ad in some newsletter at a drop-in place she went to downtown?

Well, she does and she is. Eric's Cree, she says. From that reserve out by the lake. Huh. Who knew? Not me of course, but then there's a lot that slides by me sometimes. She told me a bunch of other stuff too, which I'm probably supposed to keep to myself, so I'm not going to tell you. At least not now, but it's interesting. It's way unique compared to my boring life. Kind of makes me see Deena a little differently. She's pretty cool. I like her aunt.

So, see? I'm making friends just like I said before! Just thought you'd want to know. Catch ya later!!

ChapterSixteen

We sat there in that kitchen for an hour, soaking up the sun through the kitchen window and drinking tea while Deena told me her story. Or some of her story. I'm sure there's a lot more and it's probably a lot worse than what she talked about that afternoon, but it was still pretty interesting and so completely off the wall compared to my own experience that I felt a little envious, ridiculous though that may sound. My parents might be certifiable, but they're also predictable, boring and stable, which in turn makes my life boring, at least to me. And they're both always there, which I should be seeing as a plus, I suppose, but which feels drab.

"I don't remember her at all," Deena said softly, talking about her mother. "Nothing. I remember a very old lady, but just barely."

Mel said, "She remembers her grandma, her mom's mom. She died, too. A long time ago."

"And my dad," Deena said, "I do remember him. But mostly he's shadows and he's frightening. There are other people around and I can't make out their faces. That's really about it. Until I got to the foster place and started school. That's when my memories start."

At this point, my chin was practically on the table and I made an effort to swallow and look less shocked. "Both my parents are alive," I said lamely. "And well. Or as well as they ever are. Where's your dad?"

"Gone," Deena said shortly.

"Where?" My mind couldn't quite work its way around the concept of someone simply vanishing as if they'd never existed. "Where'd he go?"

Mel spoke up. "We don't know, Ari. When people want to disappear, it's not that difficult. Especially if they're not living regular lives with regular jobs."

She stopped and cleared her throat, obviously trying to decide how much to say. "If they're making their money off the streets somehow and they don't want to be found, they can vanish into another city or province quite easily. Take a different name. Live rough on the streets anywhere."

"Y'mean, like selling dope and stuff?" I was a little out of my league, but at the same time I'm not completely unaware of the hard realities around me. I've seen some pretty messed-up kids at school, and of course some of Mom's clients are as wacky as they come.

"Yes, or selling stolen goods. Or bodies." She looked straight at me, her eyes warm but sad at the same time, her voice low. "Deena was probably very lucky. She was taken from her father when she was quite young. Her siblings were older. We have no real idea of what happened to either of them, but we're hoping for the best. You know that there have been many unsolved murders, particularly of native women, and that is something we're always aware of. We haven't been able to locate Deena's brother or her sister. Yet." And her voice reached a different level as she added, "We're not giving up, Deena and me. We'll find them."

I sat there absorbing some of what Mel had said, stunned at the courage it must take just to wake up some mornings and a little annoyed at myself for having lived such an easy life. Not that it was my fault, but it seemed for a brief second that Mom and Dad could've been a little edgier and freakier so I'd have grown up less naïve. Even so, there were still some pretty basic things I was wondering about.

"So you lived in a foster place? When? Where? How'd you end up in school?"

Deena glanced over at me and then at Mel. It was obvious she couldn't decide whether to just insist I go home and get out of her life, or actually answer my questions. Maybe I was being nosy, which I'm sure is what she thought at the time, but they were really just legit questions. The kind an interviewer might ask.

"Eric and I grew up in a group home and in different foster places." Deena spoke slowly. "We met when I was really small. I've known him all my life; I can't remember a time before knowing him."

"I bet he was really cute when he was little." Seemingly, I couldn't help myself from opening my mouth and becoming a complete dork and, catching her expression, I immediately regretted my comment.

"He was about seven maybe," she continued stiffly, "and we lived with a bunch of other kids and these sort of group parents for a while. I was about five, maybe. Four? I don't even know. Then I got sent to a foster home and Eric got in trouble and ended up in a different, bigger group home in another part of the city. We didn't see each other again 'til I was about 10. The foster places didn't work out for me. There were several of them."

Her voice had a numb, unfeeling sound to it, and for once I didn't know what to say. I was actually sorry I'd ever brought the subject up.

She shook her head as if shaking her thoughts into order and continued. "We were both in the same special class and then we were back in the group home for troubled kids." She made a face. "We were troubled, all right. So," she sighed again, "we were there for a couple of years 'til he took off. And there were more foster homes. You don't really want to hear this, do you?"

"Yes!"

"Fine!" she spat. "We met Joe and Carl in one of the homes. They're older. That was their last foster family and then when they moved out, Eric went too. And eventually, I moved on, too. I didn't see him again until we ran into him at that drugstore."

"What about that pregnant lady?" I asked. "You know, the one Eric talked about?"

"The last foster place. She was OK, then her boyfriend moved in and she got pregnant and kicked us out. Probably better that way."

Deena was staring at the floor and she finally glanced up at me. "That's it," she said, sounding a little angry. "Satisfied?"

Well sort of. In a way, I guess. I mean, I was satisfied that she'd told me her story. I was also a bit shaken up by her story. If the truth be admitted, I was completely blown away by her story. Her bravery amazed me, but at the same time, I had absolutely no idea what to say to her.

I could picture her as a little kid, tattered running shoes, grubby hands, and completely at the mercy of every adult. How do you hug the hurting, sad little girl inside the almost grown-up girl? Would that little girl even want you to hug her? Maybe she'd think it was an insult or something, which would make matters worse. My heart can feel like a closed fist at times like these when all kinds of possibilities present themselves, but fear plows in and shuts down everything that feels softer.

Furthermore, there was still the matter of whether or not she was a rival for Eric's affections. I'm shallow. I admit it.

"Well, yeah," I said. "I'm satisfied, I guess."

"You guess?" She was truly offended now. "I've told you things I've never shared with anyone but Auntie Mel, and you 'guess' you're satisfied?"

Some instinct told me I'd basically screwed up. "You must be a lot older than me," I said suddenly, the math – thank you, Mr. Steed – racing through my brain. "If Eric's around 25, then you . . ."

"How can you even think about that right now?" She stared at me, horrified. "Who cares how old I am or how old Eric is! Don't you get it?"

"But we're lucky, right kiddo?" Mel had been silent through most of this, sipping her tea and gazing out the window at the flowers on the patio. She stood now and looped an arm around Deena's shoulders, giving her a massive hug that lifted her off her chair. "We found each other! That was a wonderful day, that one."

Deena smiled and shrugged, shy in front of me, then hugged Mel back. Her eyes had brightened when she turned back to speak to me. "Our culture has tentacles," she said, "just like an octopus. A lady at a community outreach knew a lady, who knew a lady, who knew a lady . . ." Her voice trailed off.

"Who knew me!" Mel said triumphantly. "And that was my lucky day."

She left the room then, glancing back and telling me to drop by again.

"She's gotta go to work," Deena said. "And I've got homework."

Which I took as my cue to leave. And which is also when every little thing I knew and loved and believed in decided to totally mess with my mind and complicate my entire life, a life that up until then had been based on the simple premise of avoiding Mom. I hate it when all my preconceived notions come crashing down and make me have to rethink everything. It's so annoying. And this thing that happened next actually left me questioning not only my sanity, but also my physical well-being. I mean, maybe I was really sick or something and didn't

even know it! Maybe that's why all of it happened. My guard
was down, because I was sick. Or not. It's hard to say.

ChapterSeventeen

It came about because I took a nap. Amazing how one little decision that seems so minor at the time can lead to such major complications later on.

When I got home from Deena's I could hear Mom rattling around in the kitchen. My ultimate goal being to avoid having to help her, I took a run at the stairs and tore up to my room before she could so much as open her mouth to call my name. Once in my room, with my music plugged in and a really boring bio textbook in hand, lying on my bed, it was a simple step to just let my eyes drift shut and escape from reality.

Problem was that the sleep in itself, although totally refreshing, was also incredibly strange and almost impossible to describe. Especially since it involved voices, tribespeople, odd smells, intense cold and confusing questions that didn't seem to have answers.

I realize listening to other people describe their dreams in mind-numbing detail is repulsive, but the most impressive thing about this dream was it wasn't a dream! It wasn't anything like a dream. It was for real, although it happened while I was sleeping and so normal people would call it a dream. Which is where I realize I'm going to run into difficulty, because there isn't a word for what this was. I could make up a word, I guess: 'floggle.' It was a floggle!!

What happened was this: I was standing in the middle of a rushing stream. It was actually me looking down at my body and washing myself, and although the stream was really cold and my mind knew it was cold, it actually didn't feel cold to me, because the person I was didn't know anything different from this stream. It was where we got our water and it was what it was. I could see my feet in the water and I could accept the coldness the way a deer or a horse might. It was simply the place where we washed ourselves. So, unlike my current self, I wasn't wishing the water was warm or in a Jacuzzi or had bubbles, and I wasn't judging it in any way. It just was.

And in the back of my mind I knew there was a group of people beyond the banks and trees and I felt solid and good knowing I belonged with that group, but this was a special day, so I was washing. I can still see my legs and feet in the water and my hands scooping up to wash my upper body and face. I was a man. Middle-aged. And I have no idea what my face looked like, because I had never seen my face.

And then, at that precise moment of my hands scooping up splashing water, I opened my eyes again in my own bed, my book on my chest, my music still playing and for a long couple of seconds I had no idea who I was. I was barren. Empty. Everything in my head was gone. No vowels, no words, no idea of where I was or who I was. Nothing. A vacuum.

The experience was remarkable for its vast nothingness. It only lasted a few seconds, maybe five seconds, and yet it was such an immense sense of blank unknowing that it totally freaked me out. As soon as I started to realize there was nothing in my memory I started to freak, but then my sense of who I am came back. I remembered my name and my parents and friends and the place where I live and I was back in my life, but before that for those five seconds my whole being was just gone. I was empty. Weird. It was very weird to have a brain that suddenly is empty of any personal knowing. I'm not talking about 'drawing a blank,' which is something that happens to me quite often, particularly in math class; I'm talking not existing at all. Cool. But I hope it doesn't happen again.

Which is when a soft, warm and quietly deep voice spoke up and calmly said, 'what was your face before you were born?' and because the voice spoke directly into my left ear I actually turned my face to see who was there. Of course there was nobody there.

And that's when Mom hollered up the stairs from the kitchen, asking for some help down there before everyone arrives, and just like dust settling back down after it's been disturbed, all my thoughts and ideas and knowledge of being Ari and in my room in my house all came back into my head and heart and I felt heavier somehow, as if all this knowledge had weight of its own.

ChapterEighteen

Facebook: Between you and M. Collins
02-21-Yearofourlordwhatever

You probably think I'm going to blab on at great length about what happened tonight, but I'm not. Mom would literally kill me if I told you anything really private about the readings she does. So therefore I can't describe all the horrendous junk that went on with Sara and Brandi, and what they said and how they acted and what an annoying person Sara can be, but it was certainly dramatic. The night turned out to be an impressive 10.5 on the freaky scale, and it's no doubt gonna cause a ton of problems for me.

Mom insists that we all make our own reality. Scary thought! She's constantly ruminating aloud about whether our life is a dream or our dreams are our lives, a line of reasoning that always tends to give me a headache. She quotes a Japanese guy from way back, some guy named Tzu, who evidently had a dream about butterflies and then when he woke up he wrote a Buddhist tract wondering if he was a man dreaming of butterflies or actually a butterfly dreaming of being a man. These are the kinds of discussions we have at my house. The ones that drive me absolutely crazy. It can't be normal. Did you used to talk about stuff like that with your mother? Is it Mom who's crazy or is it me?

OMG. I'm starting to think like that Tzu guy. Time to take a
break. Ttyl. Maybe. Maybe not. This blogging thing might
not be such a good idea. Anyway, that's it for now.

The grogginess and sense of unreality, of being unmoored,
like a balloon floating over trees and fences with a loose string
dangling, had finally dissipated. My feet were still cold from
standing in that stream, but I mostly knew again who and where
I was. And I felt at home in my body, which was nice, because
at first it felt like foreign territory. I couldn't seem to recognize
my body or my self. Looking down at my arms and legs, it had
felt like I'd gotten 'dressed' in a body that I picked out, similar to
the way I'd pick out a T-shirt to wear for the day. Only the fear of
Mom getting wind of what happened and then celebrating like
a madwoman because I had some kind of out-of-body experience had kept me up and moving around and acting as normal
as possible.

For me, wrapped in my fantasy world of drugstore romance
and the crazy energy of my nap incident, the dreaded psychic
evening with two of the G6 had become pretty much a non-
event. This obliviousness had helped the remainder of the
afternoon pass in a relatively painless way, but that painless-
ness was also a curse since it meant I was caught off-guard
when the doorbell rang and Mom called out for me to answer it.

We'd spent what was left of the afternoon wrapping dough
around little vegetarian wieners and cutting squares of cheese,
while she rambled on about guides and Deena, and I dreamed
of a little apartment and Eric. When the bell rang, she was in
the living room lighting candles and incense and I was doodling
around on a notepad in the kitchen drawing smiley faces,
completely unconscious of the time.

"Hi!" Sara and Brandi blew past me, craning their necks in
every direction, breathing it all in through their foreign noses,

avidly taking in the sights like a busload of tourists heading into an exotic museum.

"Hi." I was less effusive.

"C'mon in," I added unnecessarily, since they were not only already inside, but also had taken off their jackets and were busily padding around my living room in their sock feet.

"You have a very interesting house," Sara gushed in an enthusiastically false voice to Mom. "Very different. Is it supposed to be retro?" She fingered the drapes. "It's not at all like my house. My mother likes things new and clean."

"Well, thank you," Mom said, completely missing Sara's pointed sarcasm, as she continued lighting candles and wandering through her own foggy world. "We've tried to stay true to our intuitive voices."

A groan burbled through me as I opened the door again, for Deena this time, but I caught the sideways glance Brandi threw at Sara and for a second I hated her for it. That sideways glance told me they'd be discussing all this later on. And not discussing it in some mature, generous fashion, but totally dissecting it in a really nasty 'did-you-see-the-salt-under-the-window-frames' way.

"Deena!" Mom beamed. "I'm so glad you could come."

"Oh!" Sara looked up from the bowl of potpourri she'd been examining and I could sense a note of uncertainty behind her naturally bossy tone. "I didn't think anyone else would be here tonight. I thought this was a private reading. Just me and Brandi."

"Deena needs to be a part of this," Mom asserted in that blandly emphatic way she has of pulling a statement out of thin air as if it's so obviously something everyone should know. "Tonight is really for her benefit. All the energies came together for a purpose."

"Well, I'm not paying for her reading," Sara began defiantly, and then added in a slightly more conciliatory tone, "Not that I don't want to or anything, but I really only came with enough money for me and Brandi. And besides, I'm the one that booked

you! I'm the one you said had somebody right behind me.
Remember? Remember how I asked and you said I did?"

I'm no wizard, but I could see the thoughts flooding her brain.
She was intent on standing her ground – acquiring what she'd
planned on purchasing while ordering the paid help around. And
yet, at the same time, she wanted to be careful when the paid
help in this case claimed to have connections to the spirit world.
Who knew what kind of eerie things might happen if you bossed
around a representative of the spirit world unnecessarily?

"I understand, and this won't cost you anything extra," Mom
assured her. "Deena is here as my guest. Now take your seats,
ladies. Over here on the sofa." She motioned toward our couch.
"Or in a chair. Anywhere you feel comfortable."

Our sofa is a second-hand one passed down from an ancient
aunt, who died when I was a baby and who evidently only sat
on it on her birthday or something, which left it in 'excellent
condition' according to Mom. 'Free condition,' according to
Dad, whose often-stated goal is to not spend one skinny dime
if he can avoid it and who at that moment was in the kitchen
puttering around with the teapot and getting ready to put snacks
on the coffee table when the reading was over.

All I know is the sofa, while comfortable, is also pink. Dark
cherry pink, covered with a disturbingly lush garden of light
pink roses and huge green leaves. Mom has tried to disguise its
general ugliness, which even she has acknowledged is night-
marish, by throwing pillows all over it, but there's no disguising
the outrageous riot of those roses. They often seem to glow with
a creepy alien life of their own, as if when people aren't around
they're busy propagating and making more horrific baby roses.

Mom was talking to Brandi. "You need to use the sofa, young
lady, and feel free to put extra pillows behind your back. I know
how achy it's been lately."

Brandi tossed another look Sara's way and settled herself gingerly on the edge of the couch as instructed, but Sara was so busily intent on searching for a spot to sit that didn't involve too close a proximity to Deena, she missed the glance. I saw it though, and I knew what it meant: Brandi was freaked out by Mom already, and things hadn't even begun yet. I heaved a sigh and chose the chair. Curled in the corner of our overstuffed rocker I could keep an eye on everyone, ready to pounce into action if need be, but still stay out of the action myself.

When everyone had settled, Mom pulled a little purple velvet bag from her pocket and emptied her collection of rune stones onto the wooden coffee table.

There was a long silent pause while Mom breathed in deeply several times and cleared the air out of her lungs again with a forceful whooshing sigh. Her eyes were half-closed, hands cupped open, spine straight and head tilted back. Her hair fell in a long copper sheet over her shoulders and back.

"OK." She settled herself more firmly on a cushion across from where Deena sat cross-legged on the floor. She turned a rune over and ran her forefinger along its carved image.

"We are ready to begin. I hope everyone is comfortable." Her voice changed slightly, growing softer and deeper as she spoke, her tone becoming rhythmic and almost hypnotic. She placed her hands on her knees, palms upward and drew in a deep breath.

"I invite only positive entities and affirmative spirits to prevail here tonight," she said slowly and distinctly. "I invoke loving protection for all in this room. Nothing will harm us. We are completely safe. Only positive energy will enfold us. Each of us is surrounded by a white and protective light. A caring light. This light allows love to permeate, but guards our safety by blocking anything negative or destructive."

She waited a moment and then, her voice in a soft singsong, she spoke to Sara and Brandi. "We can begin now. What have you girls come here tonight to ask about?"

Gently, almost lovingly, she touched each rune in turn, absently turning one this way, and one another, gazing down at the blocks with a distracted trancelike look on her face, while waiting for a response. She rested her fingertips lightly for an instant on one stone before shifting it to her right and then reaching out to trace the design on another.

The faint click of the little tiles as Mom shuffled them around was the only sound in the room as everyone sat back waiting for someone else to make the first move. She allowed the silence to settle and waited patiently for someone to speak.

ChapterNineteen

Sara cleared her throat, the noise suddenly abrasive and a little surprising in the peaceful quiet.

"So, is this how we start?" she asked plaintively. "Like, doesn't something else happen? Like, maybe voices or something? Or is this all there is?"

Mom glanced up from her stones, her eyes lingering on each face in turn before stopping at Sara's. "Yes, dear," she said to Sara. "This is how it works. Go ahead. Ask your questions."

"Oh . . ." She trailed off. It was a novel experience to hear the uncertainty in Sara's voice. "I didn't know we had to ask you questions. I guess I just thought you'd tell us things. Tell us what's going to happen. Like a crystal ball or something."

In preparation for the reading, Mom had grouped candles around the room in varying combinations of threes and fives. For added illumination, she'd lit one small lamp on the coffee table under the window and then draped a red scarf over the lampshade to soften any glare. The collective light flickered on the walls, and as I watched Brandi's expression a sort of long shadow surged up from her head, ebbing and flowing against the backdrop of the wall. It startled me. I blinked and the image disappeared.

"Questions are a way of opening the lines between us," Mom was explaining. "You ask me something and then my guides give me messages. Sometimes the question you ask has nothing to do with why you're really here, but it gives us a starting point."

"We're not gonna see ghosts or anything are we?" Brandi burst out. She was trying to keep the fear out of her voice, trying to sound in-charge and cool, but her dread was so obvious in the little tremor that even I could hear it.

Deena glanced up as Brandi spoke and I saw her exchange a quick look with Mom.

"No ghosts," Mom assured. "Only a few insights, hopefully, and because I always request that all who enter here be secure and safe, you have no reason to fear anything, Brandi. Just relax. Be open. We all need to remain positive and open in order for the energies to come through as clearly as possible."

"So are you gonna tell us the future?" Sara was trying to pin things down. Until tonight I hadn't fully realized how she liked to control things. Good luck, I thought, trying to tell Mom she has to stick to anybody else's program. "Can you tell us when we're going to get married or when we're going to die?"

Mom sighed and looked straight into Sara's eyes. "Even if I could, I wouldn't tell you those things," she stated. "We are going to concentrate on being open to whatever messages our guides feel are important for us in the lives we are living at this moment.

"Nothing else," she spoke forcefully, "and nothing negative. Only things that the guides feel will advance our spiritual growth. We need to trust the messages that come through and not argue or bring anything negative to the experience. This is about your intuition, your soul, and not about your brain."

Keeping 'open' and non-judgmental was going to be easier said than done, I thought as I watched Brandi battle her fear and uncertainty. A candle flickered when the furnace kicked in and she gave a nervous little jump, and then forced herself to settle back on the couch cushions, her shoulders stiff and her fists tightly clenched on her lap.

Sara broke the quiet again, ready to do battle with Mom. "OK, here's my question: Does Steven love me?" Her voice was brazen, loaded with defiance.

Mom's eyes rested for a moment on an area above Sara's head, then she moved a rune to one side and said casually, "That's not the question you're here to ask, but I'll answer it for you anyway. The question you are wanting to ask is very different.

"You already know he doesn't love you, not in the way you're thinking he should. He has many obstacles ahead in his life. I'm seeing a long string with frayed ends and many, many knots. Knots upon knots. Very complicated and difficult to unravel. This boy has a lot of challenges ahead of him."

"String?" Sara was so obviously disappointed that I nearly laughed. "You see a string?"

"Psychics all work in different ways," Mom explained. Her patience impressed me, reluctantly I'll admit, since I'm not used to viewing her positively, but still it was a novel and kind of nice feeling. As my first time watching her in action, this was turning out to be sort of cool.

"In my case I see symbols," she went on. "I sense presences or energies around my clients. I get an impression of colour and a very strong awareness of information. The pictures I get in my mind help me understand and guide the people who come to me for help."

Deena's face had flushed to a warm pink while Mom spoke, and she said quietly, "Where do I go next?"

"I'm not done!" Sara cried. "This is my reading, Deena! Mine and Brandi's." She turned to Mom. "Tell me what the question is then – the one you think I came here to ask about." Her tone was challenging.

"I'm not sure how you'd phrase the question," Mom began, and at Sara's disbelieving snort, she carried on, "but I do know the answer." She looked straight at Brandi now. "I'm seeing a young female essence," she said. "Behind your left shoulder and slightly above you.

"This baby you are carrying will be a girl. If you choose to have her. You still have a little time to decide."

Mom sat quietly, her eyes focused on the middle distance. It was all I could do to breathe normally, and my throat was so dry it felt cracked. I couldn't look at Brandi, but Sara's wide eyes told me all I needed to know. Mom was so intent on whatever messages she was receiving that she didn't seem to notice the tension piling up in the room.

After a long in-breath, she said, "This little girl will bring you great joy. And also great pain. I see that the father will not be around. Wait. Not quite."

She was listening to something no one else could hear, and I felt a tingle go down my spine.

"He won't be around until much later," she said. "When the child is maybe 10 or 12 years old, he'll come back into your life. She's very cute. She's a kid who loves sports and she's always on a team of some sort. I see lots of scraped knees and bumps. I see a lot of turmoil. Dust clouds of emotional stuff. This is a long period of great growth for you, if you choose to use it. It will also be a period of pain and with that pain, huge amounts of anger at the people around you."

Mom waved her hands through the air as if brushing away a swarm of insects.

"Clouds of negative energy surround you," she said. "You can choose to learn through this negativity and turn that energy clear, or you can choose not to. It's up to you. All of it is yours to choose every step of the way."

"Will we get married?" Brandi whispered.

"No." Mom's voice was firm. "You each marry someone else, but in your case not for many years. The father of this girl will disappear from your life very soon. There will be lots of heated voices coming at you. They come from him and from others. I see many mouths opening and lots of harsh explosions, so that means lots of angry words. You wait a long time before marrying. And there are no other children for you."

The rest of us remained silent, caught up in the moment. The feeling of electricity in the room was palpable. The air seemed to tingle.

Mom continued quietly. "There are no rights or wrongs here, Brandi. The choice of whether or not to carry this child is entirely up to you. Her entity will understand, whichever way you choose to go. However, as in every choice, every decision we make in life, what you do in this case will have ongoing repercussions for you and for others as you go through your lifetime. You will learn different lessons and attract different people into your life depending upon the choices you make."

I risked a glance across the circle and was amazed at the change in Deena. Her eyes had closed, and her hands were cupped open on her thighs. She seemed to be in a trance of her own.

"Deena." Mom's voice was so soft I could barely hear it. "Place your hands on Brandi's back. Brandi, turn please and lie on your side."

What amazed me most was that both of them actually did what she was suggesting. Sara glared across the circle of candlelight at me and I shrugged back. She threw herself back against her chair and crossed her arms. Her leg jiggled with frustration. Neither of us spoke.

I watched as Deena got up, knelt at the side of the sofa and gently placed the palms of her hands on Brandi's shirt just above her waist. She rested them there briefly, and then moved her hands out and slightly away from Brandi's back, stopping when the palms were several centimetres away.

"Do you feel the heat?" Mom asked.

"Yes," both answered at once, and Brandi gave a little shudder.

"What is that?" she asked. The tremor was back in her voice and Mom leaned forward and placed a hand on Brandi's shoulder.

"Deena's hands have powers, they're like a conduit," she said slowly. "Your back has been aching and keeping you awake at night. The ache comes from your inner emotional turmoil, not from anything physically wrong with you. You need to tell your parents."

"I can't." Brandi began sobbing. "I can't tell them. They'll kill me."

Figuratively speaking, I thought, because obviously, they wouldn't actually kill her. They'd probably be plenty pissed off though. Judging by her clothes and the other stuff she's always got with her, Brandi's family had a lot more money than mine, and therefore more to lose as well, at least in their own minds.

"My mother thinks I'm not trying hard enough at school. She's always mad and she's never home, and my Dad doesn't even call anymore." Her voice had reached a higher pitch, loaded with tears. "He lives downtown, but he never even calls. It's like he's forgotten all about me. I can't talk to them!"

"Who can you talk to?" Mom's voice was gentle. "Find someone you can trust, and do it quickly."

The room was quiet now, except for Brandi's stifled crying, and then, as I stared at where Deena still knelt next to Brandi, a surge of bright purple blew out from Deena's palms, so thick it appeared nearly solid, like very light cotton fabric. As I watched, the colour ebbed into a pale, powdery blue and then grew in intensity to brilliant lilac again, throbbing against Brandi's shirt.

Suddenly, I wished we could turn on all the lights and maybe the TV too, just to dispel the heaviness in the atmosphere. I don't normally get creeped out, having grown up in the craziness surrounding my Mom, but this was different.

This was Deena, a person I'd thought of as not only normal, but also slightly pathetic in a way, someone who would be grateful to have me or anyone else as a friend. And now to find she had some kind of weird mystical healing power was unsettling to say the least. And to realize on top of it all, that it seemed I was developing some kind of nutty ability to see energy, or wander out of my life and into another one at the drop of a hat, was just one more reason to call this whole experiment in G6 paranormal junk off.

"That's it!" The words burst out of me under their own initiative. "That's it, Mom! Enough! This is over. Time for Sara and Brandi to head home."

Although it wasn't late, it had grown dark by the time I flipped out and ordered them to leave. Mom switched on the outside light and offered a ride home, but Brandi and Sara declined in unison and scurried down the walk together, practically joined at the hip, leaving me to sag against the door frame watching them go, while Dad wandered into the room carrying a tray with our post-reading snacks and a pot of herbal tea.

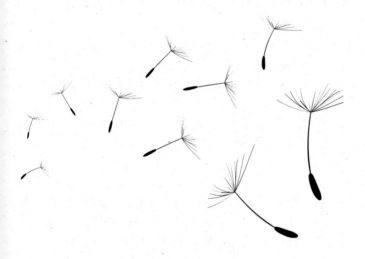

Chapter Twenty

After they'd left, Mom went through the room cleansing the atmosphere again, returning it to its natural state of hippy-chic, clapping her hands, focusing on keeping the air molecules positive and thanking the presences only she could see. She removed the scarf from the table lamp and then sat heavily on the sofa, her bare feet tucked up under her and a steaming cup of tea in hand.

"Deena," she began, "what you have is a gift. Your hands have healing powers."

"It hurts. My hands hurt when I do it." Deena took a piece of cheese from the tray Dad proffered and, worming her way across the floor, she leaned against the sofa, her back to where Mom sat. "The palms of my hands tingle, like a million little pointy pins. They feel cold, icy, and like they belong to someone else. Everyone says my hands are so hot, but to me they're freezing cold. I have no control over them. It isn't fun."

"Do you have visions or hear voices?" Mom asked.

"All I do is let them go wherever they want to go. I don't try to figure out where they should be. My head seems to disappear. There's a light that comes between me and the other person."

"Do you feel energized afterwards?" Mom sounded more like she was leading the conversation somewhere, rather than actually asking a question.

Deena took a long time in answering. "Yes," she said finally.

"Gifts such as yours are rare," Mom said. "They need to be shared. As you grow in awareness, you'll find the energy strengthening and becoming more accurate with each experience. And as you gain experience it will become less uncomfortable for you physically."

"I'm not sure I want this so-called gift," Deena muttered. "All my life I've been different and I'm sick of it. I just want to be normal."

It was a longing I could definitely identify with, having had that same yearning for most of my life.

"But you're not normal," Mom said reasonably. "Nobody ever is. What is 'normal' anyway? Look at Brandi tonight. Many people would consider her life to be a lucky one and envy her."

At this point Mom glanced meaningfully at me and I looked away.

"Instead," Mom continued, "she's got heaps of trouble and growth in front of her. It's her path, her walk and we can't condemn or judge; all we can do is watch her walk and help if we can. I don't know if it's 'normal' or not, but it's what she's chosen to put in front of herself. There are reasons for this happening and it may lead to her growing in depth and compassion. Or it may not. It's entirely up to her."

Mom paused for a sip of tea and then continued. "Once you accept this aspect of yourself, Deena, you'll find peace, and with that peace an enormous sense of strength. Be open, Deena, open to what they're telling you, but always remain humble and thankful. This is an enormous honour."

For several moments Deena was quiet. She gazed down to where her hands were folded in her lap, seeming to view them as if they belonged to someone else. Which I could understand, since my entire body after those experiences earlier felt like a foreign place to me, like a place I'd thought I'd like to visit and now found myself actually walking the halls of. Familiar and yet strange.

"For the longest time," Deena began finally, almost as though she were talking to herself, her eyes still on the hands folded in her lap, "for so many years, all I really wanted was to wake up one morning and be white. Y'know? I wanted a TV family of my own – two parents who had coffee in the morning and argued about little things, but they belonged to me. A brother or a sister and crazy neighbours. A backyard. I wanted white skin and blond hair and a pet dog."

Mom smiled. "Me, too," she said, "although I've got the 'white' part. But really when I was a kid all I wanted was to be like every other kid. I outgrew it finally, but it wasn't easy."

It wasn't easy for me either, all this new information about Mom and Deena. It meant I was gonna have to start seeing Mom as a human being and not just the maternal unit. That was gonna take some doing.

"I decide right now." Deena spoke with authority as she accepted a cracker and cheese from Dad, who was silently listening in and chowing down. "What I want in this life, what I want more than anything, is to be my own totem."

Mom laughed at that. "What a great way of putting it!" she cried.

And I just sat there like Dad, munching cheese cubes, watching and listening while the two of them bonded like mad, as Deena talked about finding her aunt and about her foster places, all the things she'd been trying to keep private and which she now just simply opened up and poured out at my mother like some sort of golden offering to a goddess.

I remembered the time, maybe a year earlier, when I'd been absolutely over-the-top furious about something I couldn't even recall anymore, but so insanely angry that I'd finally shrieked in full-blown, red-faced rage, "I hate you! Why do you have to be so weird?" at Mom. That scene now began replaying itself through my memory in an endless, slightly tedious and embarrassing loop.

She had stayed silent for what seemed like ages, while I ranted and steamed. My face was hot, my ears felt like they were going to pop off with the frustration and stress of living with those two freaky parents of mine, and ultimately all they did was look across the table at each other, breathe deeply and then begin attempting to reassure me that anger can be a positive emotion, that it can lead to growth and artistic evolution and whatever. It was so pointless, all that anger, like beating your head against a wall or punching a cushion. It made no dent in anything.

And watching Deena and Mom right now, and thinking about Mel alone in her little house waiting for her long-lost niece to come home tonight, and missing her dead sister, it all just came to me how connected we all were even though ultimately we weren't connected at all. We were all so individual with our own very important lives. Separate on our trails through time. But still linked.

Chapter Twenty-One

Facebook: Between you and M. Collins
02-24 Yearofourlordwhatever

So I guess the Facebook experiment is officially over, and this is going to be my last post to you. I notice you've dropped the picture on your account and you've got one of those lame blue-and-white androgynous cameo profile things up instead. Kinda creepy. Don't let all this stuff turn you off the Internet, by the way, because it really is like everything else in life - there's some good, there's some bad, there's a lot of in-between. But it's fun, and you were really getting good at Googling and all. Remember the day you found the Google Maps page? That was cool for you!

It's kind of sad in a way that the principal got wind of this and threw a hissy, but on the other hand, maybe it's better. Too much information can be tough for both of us, but Mrs. C. I want you to know I honestly got to like this way of emptying myself out. Sincerely. It was good. So, thanks. And I guess I'll see you in class!

Both Sara and Brandi had left my house a lot more subdued than they'd entered it, and their visit was still on my mind as I walked into school Monday morning. Their experience at "Chateau Ari" had been a chastening one, some smug part of me gloated, but another slightly wiser part of me warned there'd be hell to pay later. Girls like them have no shame about taking out their frustrations on anyone nearby, and I already knew with a sinking heart I'd be the one nearby.

Although, it did occur to me there might be a way to exploit the inborn fear both of them seemingly had concerning anything remotely resembling otherworldly entities. As long as I reminded them regularly that I had a live-in pipeline to the land of the dead, I'd probably be safe from any truly drastic potential repercussions. In my own case, I was relieved to find a hot bath and a solid night's sleep had brought me back to my standard level of cynicism.

My main concern now was Deena, her deep secrets and all the various reasons she hadn't told me about them. Not to mention all the possible relationships she enjoyed with Eric, man of my dreams, and all the as-yet-undiscovered details that I was convinced needed to be explored in order for our friendship to deepen.

And deepen it must, since after the others had stalked off in a huff, Deena had sat with Mom and talked for what seemed like an eternity about matters dealing with the metaphysical, a subject that I still had absolutely no interest in whatsoever. It seemed to me she might be hanging around my house a lot more than might normally be expected now that she'd connected with Mom.

I approached her Monday morning at school, ready for a showdown. "So, you've got some big explaining to do, Deena!"

"Really? About what exactly?" She was rummaging through her locker and her voice was muffled.

"About what? About what?" I realized I was repeating myself, but at the same time it wasn't easy finding the right words to explain the depths of my righteous indignation. "About your stupid hands, that's what!"

Deena pulled her head out and shot me a look. She'd realized, no doubt, that I'd be difficult if not impossible to put off the track.

"My hands," she said quietly, "are my business."

"Not when you get my Mom involved, they're not," I asserted. "Then they become my business too."

"Ari," she sighed, sounding way too much like Mom for my liking, "please keep your voice down. It's not something I go around telling people. It hurts to do it. And it's exhausting."

"And that's what you do with Eric?" I exploded. "You go into his room and lay hands on his body?"

"Will you keep your voice down?" she spoke in a low and urgent undertone. "It's for healing," she said stiffly. "Not for any other reasons. For god's sake, Ari, relax! Be quiet!"

"Well, how was I to know that?"

It was an outrage. All these spooky goings-on involving not only Mom, but now Deena as well. It was as if they had joined forces against me.

"I'm no mind reader!" I snapped. "I only know what I see with my own two eyes, and what I saw that day was you and Eric going into his bedroom together."

"And from that you assumed we had something going on?" Deena was as outraged as I; that much was obvious. "You better start learning to mind your own business, Ari, or someone is really going to tear you apart someday."

"Oh, and that someone is you, I suppose!" Nobody threatens me. "Don't even start with me, Deena!"

"Why would you care anyway?" she asked. "What difference could it possibly make to you what Eric and I do?"

This was hitting too close to home for comfort. Time to get her off the trail. A very smooth operation was called for here. Diplomacy. Tact.

"I'm in love with him!" I blurted out and then clapped a hand over my mouth. "No! No, I'm not!" I was backpedaling as fast as humanly possible. "Not really. Maybe a little."

Deena was watching me with a very peculiar expression on her face. If I hadn't known better, I'd have described it as sympathy.

"I am not in love with Eric." I forced myself to speak clearly. Calmly. Slowly. I started again. "I don't know what made me say that, but I don't *love* him. I like him. I think he's really cute." I could feel a look of dreamy wonder begin to work its way across my face.

"Really, really cute," I whispered in an effort to convince her of the opposite. "And he has a very nice body. Nice lips; I love the way he smiles."

Catching myself in mid-drool, so to speak, I quickly spun my wheels, metaphorically speaking of course, and made an abrupt left turn. "But I'm not in love with him. That was a mistake. A mistake on my part. An overstatement."

Deena was staring at me with a look of pure dismay.

"You know," she said slowly, "Eric is one of my very closest friends."

"I know! Best friends, yes, I get it!" I was babbling and couldn't seem to stop myself. "I understand. He's taken. Totally understand. No worries."

Deena had been waiting patiently for me to be finished, and now she said, "He's one of my friends." She was emphatic. "And because he's my friend, I can tell you right now he'd be . . ."

"Completely wrong for me." I finished the sentence for her. "I know. Mom has already pointed that out about a million times. Completely wrong and way too old. I get it, Deena."

"Will you please shut up for a minute? Just let me finish a sentence!"

Well, nearly everyone I've ever known in my life has asked, or even demanded, that I shut up, so hearing it come from Deena shouldn't have been the shock it was. This was Deena speaking, though. Deena, whose normal behaviour is so quiet and self-effacing she might as well be a ghost. Which is why hearing her talk that way made such an immediate impression and I actually did shut up. Well, not shut up in physical terms, since my mouth was actually hanging open, but I did stop speaking.

"OK," she sighed. "Eric is like a brother. Wait!" Deena held up a hand to stop me from interrupting. "Sort of a messed-up brother, anyway. My own brother is lost to me. I don't know where he is anymore. But Ari, Eric is not the most stable person in the world."

Right. As if my parents represented 'stable.' My life had been one long gong show since the day I was born.

"Yeah, but 'stable''s kind of boring, don't you think?" I said. "I mean, my life is already boring enough. I'd like to have some excitement."

"Ari, a guy like Eric has a lot of stuff to deal with. He went through a lot of trouble growing up and he's going to need lots of time to learn who he is before he can really be good for anyone else. He's pretty selfish and a little bit careless."

Maybe I'd be good for him, I thought. Bring some 'stability' to his life. Poor guy. He needed me. I could help make up for all the pain of his childhood and make him laugh and feel wanted.

"So, maybe it'd be good for him to have a girlfriend like me," I stated. "Someone who has a 'stable' home life, with 'stable' parents and a mature attitude." I caught her rolling her eyes and I stressed, "I do have a mature attitude! You just haven't noticed."

She laughed aloud there in the hallway, and several people by their lockers looked over before turning back to their own conversations.

"Ari," she sputtered. "Aunt Mel was right, you're pretty funny."

"I'm not, though!" I protested. "Not funny. I'm totally serious. What if Eric's actually interested in me, then do you think it'd work?"

"Come on." She ignored my question. "Time for Bio. Let's go. Move it."

Chapter Twenty-Two

It should have come as no surprise, I suppose, since life basically makes no sense whatsoever, when Eric showed up at school that afternoon just as Deena and I were running the gauntlet through the mobs of kids hanging around the front doors of the place.

"Hey, Ari-Canary!" he greeted me and threw a brotherly arm around my shoulders.

Well, I've been called worse things, I thought, and laughed cheekily when I caught Deena narrowing her eyes at me.

"Hi, Eric," I said, his arm still around my shoulders and the wondering gaze of half the student population on us.

"You gonna talk this Deena chick into doing my elbow for me?" he teased, and even the knowledge he was basically using me as a sort of wedge in the closing door of Deena's isolation didn't faze me. At that point I really couldn't have cared less what Eric's motives were, as long as he kept that warm arm around me.

"Maybe we can convince her," I answered coyly, "if we talk nice." I grinned again in a fakely cheery way at Deena and she snorted.

"Eric, get your hands off her," she ordered, and when he immediately dropped his arm and stepped away I shot her a look designed to let her know just how close she was to losing her one and only friend in the school.

"Come on." She continued to thread her way through the mob. "Let's get out of here."

"And then you'll fix my elbow?"

"Yes, Eric, I'll look at your elbow, but keep your voice down." It was a recurring refrain I was starting to get used to hearing.

"Keep your voice down," I mimicked. "Don't let anyone know what's going on. Keep all the deep dark secrets. Blah, blah, blah."

For my pains I got a quelling look from Deena and a snort of laughter from Eric.

We were making our way through the parking lot and he kicked at a pebble. He walked with his hands in his pockets, his long braid of hair hanging straight down his back, jingling his keys and whistling off-key.

Deena cast a long look in my direction, tsked at the look of adoration I could feel on my face, and stopped under a tall, spreading elm at the far corner of school property. "Let's see the arm," she ordered.

He lifted his left elbow and she sat cross-legged on the ground, pulling him down beside her. It was an odd experience, but somehow since our discussion in the hallway, seeing her touch Eric didn't even bother me. Not much, anyway.

Shrugging off her backpack, Deena dropped his arm and held her palms together in front of her, rubbing them gently together, and then moving them apart slowly. Her focus had switched from Eric and me, and the world around her, to centre on the force she so obviously sensed between her hands. She gazed intently at the space sandwiched between her palms and, as Eric and I watched, she brought them back to within a hand's breadth of each other and palpitated the air between them as if massaging an invisible balloon.

Eric looked over at me and raised one eyebrow. He grinned. Cool, he mouthed soundlessly.

But I was too busy with my own sensations to respond.

The tree trunk behind him had suddenly taken on an unexpected life all its own, and I felt my mouth droop open as a swirl of nearly visible power hummed around the trunk of the tree, soaring up until it encompassed the entire canopy. Small eddies of bluish electrical force burst out of each pore.

It was like watching water. There was a blending of light and an unfocussed liquid-type feeling to the experience. Almost like a dream where you find yourself with shreds of a disappearing sensation that you can't quite grasp hold of other than certain specific images. But then again it was totally unlike dreams, because there was an absolute certainty that I was not dreaming; I was experiencing the sensation of light and movement all around and through that tree.

It throbbed with life and colour. Bright electrical impulses jumped in a vibrating beat from every leaf and branch. A glow of energy encompassed the entire thing and spread out to the grass beneath. Each twig, each leaf, every inch of bark was enclosed within a pulsating frisson cocoon of electrical impulse.

Chapter Twenty-Three

"Hi!" Voices broke through the bewildering swirl of motion in front of my dazed eyes and I blinked hard to dispel the images.

Like a pack of ravaging greyhounds unleashed on a rabbit, Sara, Brandi and Tiffani and a group of their hangers-on converged upon our spot under the tree, disrupting the peace, tossing their backpacks down and generally slavering all over the place. Deena abruptly dropped her hands into her lap and Eric groaned aloud.

"My friggin' elbow," he groused quietly at me. "Crap, man."

'Crap, man,' was right, I thought. There was something in the air when Deena concentrated like that, and now I found I missed it. Resentment boiled up in me.

"Hey, Deena." Sara has a personality like a bowling ball. "What exactly did you do Saturday night? To Brandi, remember?"

"I'm not sure what you're talking about." Deena's face had closed up, her cheekbones standing out stark against her skin. She shook her hair forward, until it covered half her face like some sort of camouflage.

"Come on, tell everybody!" Like that bowling ball, Sara had one object in mind and only one: to knock down whatever pins stood in her way. "Do something to me."

Deena shook her head and I said, "Hey, Sara, let it go, why don't you? She doesn't want to talk about it. Leave her alone."

"Can your Mom come over and maybe do a party at my place?" She switched her attention to me. There's just no stopping that girl once she gets going. "Maybe do readings for, like, a party or something?"

I must have showed my skepticism, because she quickly threw in, "I'll pay her of course. Her regular rate, times however many people she does readings for."

"Come on. Ask her. Please." Tiffani was looking at Deena but speaking to me.

As they spoke, Eric glanced over with such an openly confused expression I had to laugh. He almost had the same perpetually befuddled look on his face as the little Yorkie pup from down the street: all bright eyes, perky ears and general Dr. Seuss-ish appearance. Although, in Eric's case, obviously the ears and so forth were only reminiscent of Yorkie pups and not actually hairy or anything.

While I couldn't seem to keep serious, at the same time the situation was far from a laughing matter, and the thrill of him being interested enough to look confused was balanced by my conviction he'd be scared to death if he ever found out about Mom.

"What's goin' on?" he asked.

"Nothing."

"Her mom is awesome." Sara pushed her way to the front of the conversation again. "She's just so cool!"

Cool? For a second there, I thought she actually meant it.

"No, no," I assured, "just a regular van-driving mom, that's all she is. Honest."

"You are such a stick!" It was one of the hangers-on, someone whose name I always seem to forget, but she does have the most fantastic hair in school.

"Her mom," Sara said to Eric, making a melodramatic pause for emphasis, "can see into the future."

Eric looked at me again, with what seemed to my fevered imagination like new respect. Deena had apparently decided there was no fighting popular opinion, because she'd lifted his elbow and had it propped on her knee while she kneaded the air around it, moving her hands slowly down his arm and then back up again, cupping the elbow in her palms and holding it there.

"Man," he groaned, "that feels so good. It's gonna be great having you around again. Free health care, man."

It was right about then that I started to lift off. I know it's going to sound crazy, and in my own mind a certain part of me realized I was going to regret this move as long as I lived, but on the other hand it was kind of cool.

My regular body was still there, down at the tree, draped over my backpack where I reclined on the grass. Next to me was Deena, her back against the tree trunk partly for physical support and also, I suspected, for spiritual support as well. She held Eric's elbow propped against her knees and her hands were manoeuvring the air around his arm, thin threads of silver energy squiggling around his skin, her warmth a purplish haze through which the little bright white squirmy things bolted and then smoothed out.

Grouped around her were the G6, their bodies surrounded by a multicoloured cloud of conflicting energies. Radiant arms of yellow, orange, brown and pink ruptured out around them in minor explosions of irregular rhythm, the kind of rhythm you'd get if a very small and slightly outrageous kid were beating a spoon on an upturned pot. Without the sound, of course.

Interesting, I thought to myself from my new vantage point a little above and to the side of the rest of them. And then I saw Deena glance my way, her gaze moving up from my earthbound body, searching the air until she suddenly smiled brilliantly and I let out a silent whoop and grinned back.